MW00682071

Tell It Slant

Tell It Slant

a novel by

BETH FOLLETT

COACH HOUSE BOOKS

First Edition

This is a work of fiction. While Djuna Barnes appears as a
fictional character in the novel, every attempt has been made
to render truthfully certain outward particulars of her life. All
other events and persons are derived from the author's imagination.

The published work of Phillip Herring (*Djuna: The Life and
Work of Djuna Barnes*, Viking, 1995) and the Faber Library
edition of Djuna Barnes's 1936 novel *Nightwood* have been
invaluable resources during the writing of this book.

NATIONAL LIBRARY OF CANADA
CATALOGUING IN PUBLICATION DATA

Follett, Beth
    Tell it slant
1st ed.
ISBN 1–55245–081–3

        i. Title.

PS8561.O643T44 2001   C813'.54   C2001–900834–1
PR9199.3.F5648T44 2001

Edited by Alana Wilcox
Designed by Zab Design & Typography
Cover photograph by Diana Thorneycroft

Typeset in Galliard CC and printed at Coach House Printing
on bpNichol Lane, 2001.

Published with the assistance of the Canada Council for the Arts
and the Ontario Arts Council.

THE CANADA COUNCIL | LE CONSEIL DES ARTS
FOR THE ARTS | DU CANADA
SINCE 1957 | DEPUIS 1957

ONTARIO ARTS COUNCIL
CONSEIL DES ARTS DE L'ONTARIO

With infinite love
to the dead ones
for their faith
and to my mother
for life

For Justine

Tell It Slant

Tell all the Truth but tell it slant —
Success in Circuit lies
Too bright for our infirm Delight
The Truth's superb surprise
As Lightning to the Children eased
With explanation kind
The Truth must dazzle gradually
Or every man be blind —

— EMILY DICKINSON

ONE

I am drifting in the dark on night's blind waters, the vast dark volume of wet and shapeless dreams fathoms beneath me, above me a limitless sky without stars, without moon; drifting within the isotropic realm; then slowly I emerge into a lush green garden, mine or someone else's, or a yellow room expanding; a man is speaking to me while reclining on a velvet divan but I don't believe a word he says. And then some other words; and I wake into damp rumpled cotton sheets, black silk strangling my breasts, the light unfolding — grey and dim. What if I had your voice urging me like virtue? What if — words like sleep unravelling — I had walked the breadth of your voice? If words had served you? The cat stares up at me from her furrow between my thighs, no thought of time or dreams or cunning lies. A final image, brief as flame, catches like wind in a sail — your mouth not those hands with straining veins so red from hanging winter washing. Your hands, your eyes, your deep solid ineffable gaze meeting mine, what if — What if in winter those white sheets had let go and we had chased them to the frozen garden and there made a place where secrets could unfurl? And now softly crying, the dream divided, night's intention disavowed. I am tossed awake by words. I fall back upon myself.

If you had held me once in laughter. If you had spoken of the world split wide open. If the world — I rise, not wishing to wake Robin.

If mother were place not payment.

If daughter were promise.

I put on my bathrobe, go to the kitchen window and look out into this blue morning, a heavy snow beginning to fall. What is a dream? An enormous conspiring genealogy, some incest, yes, and murder. Rampant, frenzied, blind. Standing here in this moment, how the sun's first rays converge with these dreams, these rivers of words, my ancestors. How they connect to my lying next to Robin in this morning's half-light while words like pelted tomatoes smashed against the walls of my veins. A dream has its own weight, and in this simple balance I measure the night and the day.

It is said that if one were strong enough she could take the finest most powerful traits of a lost one and integrate them into herself. That if one were wise enough she could eat her dead. Trickster work. To disregard the lines and break the female body down into world without end.

Last night I jerked a suitcase across the floor of our bedroom from closet to bed, tossed in a hapless array of cotton and wool, then stood over Robin. I start this terrible day with the hope that some of my high-handed hollowness might collapse, or that I might find a door. I confess that I have blamed Robin, a useless occupation. I haven't always understood that truth wants its tempo and so today I will attempt patience. As I am forgotten in the extremity of her memory, perhaps it is possible that today I might be, from time to time, myself.

Tonight she will not come home.

The Nora Flood who is you grows up in Port Credit, about a mile inland from the lake, next door to the elementary school, and each morning you pace your washing and breakfasting and dressing to the beat of the radio program your father, Jefferson, plays. You step out the front door three minutes before nine; that way you are spared mingling in the schoolyard. It mattered then. It still matters, really. You struggle even yet, on your walks through public space, your Nikon camera in hand: *Look closer. Press deeper*. Now that everything's gone digital, you can see more clearly those schoolyard years, with their moral imperatives of ones and zeroes, of winners and losers; you have not forgotten just how you learned to be a being out of time.

She must push herself where oral expression is concerned, the teachers report as the terms drag by. My mother Myra has not been inclined to push, and on a rare occasion lies with me instead in the backyard beneath the magnolia tree where we catch its bruised pink petals in our open mouths. Myra stays home, stays out of sight mostly, working in her rose garden while I grow up alone in a dark crib and a playpen and a backyard sandbox, until my fourth birthday, when Myra gets restless and goes to work as a public health nurse. I can read Canada's Food Guide where it hangs inside a kitchen cupboard — three fruits and at least eight glasses of water a day. Myra drinks her eight glasses straight from the running tap, lips pulled back over impeccable teeth as she gulps the water down, her hair held out of the way in one clenched fist. Jefferson cannot stop her, but for me and my sisters the rule is, Use a glass. You must distinguish yourself from the animals.

Myra works in the public schools, parting heads of hair to look for lice. There's a newspaper clipping in one of her scrapbooks, Myra holding an untidy schoolboy's hand while an old doctor administers a vaccine. She's telling me she took me along in the car where I napped in the back seat while she slipped away to join up with the healing powers. What? I don't remember this. When I ask her, What else? her bath overflows and she's got to end the call. It's only six in the morning in Kitsilano; where is she hurrying to? And what is this business about healing powers?

Robin briefly nods at me over the rim of her coffee cup, an inestimable glance. She looks like death's daughter. Thoughts as indiscriminate as last night's suitcase jerk unspoken across my mind. These weekly phone calls to Myra in Vancouver were Robin's idea, calling impulsively this morning of all mornings was mine. Robin has said, Just love her for an hour here and there. The telephone receiver has the weight of a brick I want to throw.

Robin stands in the middle of the kitchen, rocking from one foot to the other. The robe she wears is torn at the armpit. I can see her breast beneath the terry cloth, can see her soft nipple hardening. Her short black hair rides high and stormy away from her forehead, her eyelids are sticky with mucus. She taps her spoon distractedly against the side of her cup.

She asks, What are your plans for tonight, Nora? She seems to need to approach the stretch of time between this question and my answer in the way of an aerial acrobat to the rope. I'm watching her, a stiffness gathering at the base of my skull. A voice in my head begins its whispering, *Please come flying*, but I don't understand it at first, it's just a bowdlerized distant singing. A severed and sudden wish for night descends upon me.

I'll call you later, I tell her, but I know I won't.

Please come flying, please come flying, these words rise up now into my mind, lettered fragments, and with these fragments the obsessive counting of minutes until I see Robin again.

Tonight she will not come home.

At twenty-two you move from Toronto to Montreal, you live in a tiny one-and-a-half above a Portuguese bakery. Graffiti on the side of the building reads: *Dehors méchant*. Your upstairs neighbour translates.

It meens de snot in your face.

How feminine the city of Montreal, you think. You are alone, without friends. You wait, and the emptiness you gather into your solar plexus is a decoy of magnificent proportions. You fill it with wine and the mechanics of taking a photograph and some anxious thoughts about time, you wait for the shape of your future to appear on the wide stretch of horizon you can see from the lookout atop Mont Royal. You wait, and while you wait you read the book *Nightwood* far into every night, shaping that Nora Flood's mouth around words you whisper to yourself in the dark, trying to reinvent your life so that you might begin to read the world.

The problems of two people seem as wide as the world to me now.

Send Robin away, whole choruses rise up in exhortation. *Trust no one*.

Last night: I lie awake in bed listening to her fumble with her key in the lock, I trace her movements along the darkened hall and into the small room where she sometimes succumbs to its divan. She draws back the heavy coats in the closet, the screech of hanger against metal rod waking the dead. She wrestles awhile with the wet and heavy wool and leather she wears. She is whispering something as she stumbles. My heart begins its night wandering: *Please come flying, please come flying*.

I remember now. This is Elizabeth Bishop, this is her invitation to Marianne Moore. Please come flying on this fine morning over the Brooklyn bridge. This is New York, and Djuna Barnes there too, in her little corner of Greenwich Village on Patchin Place, dragging small blood and her father's laughter. I am in an hour out of history, out of memory, out of imagination. Something about my conversation with Myra this morning has put this fragment of a poem again in mind. And something about the suitcase, torn open last night in haste while an almost empty bottle of red wine is kicked over, its contents draining away beneath the bed.

Strange how Myra prohibits so many notions. About flying and bridges, I mean; and other things.

I am wearing the secrets Myra gave me, and her terrible frown.

She says, What are you doing tonight? and I tell her I will call her later. But I won't call. And she will stay away. In the years we have lived together, her departures have become a steady increasing rhythm. Once I used to accompany her, into the smoky rooms where she moves from bottle to bottle, from table to table. But as time passes, I let her go alone: After a few hours, she neither remembers me nor wants me. Last night I packed a bag and stood over her, voracious, ready to eat her alive. What will it be, Robin? You choose.

She will never choose. But I take her bait every time.

You meet Robin at a New Year's Eve dance. She sits with Rae, a woman offended by love. Rae and Robin chain-smoke and share a bottle of cheap Spanish wine. Rae waves you over.

We need to learn about respect and inclusion, Robin says. All this romance. It's like we've become enamoured with death.

You might make every woman a death, Rae says, the way you refuse their hearts. I understand you. You're so critical of your lovers.

I'm critical of everything! Listen, the papers say that the time of the lesbian arguing with the world is over. Too few of us continue to perceive the world's manners as absurd. I'm one of the dangerous few, because I don't accept things.

No. You're not dangerous because you don't accept things. You're dangerous because you're blind. Take away some women's conformity and you take away their remedy.

You know this line, but it seems Robin is innocent of it.

That's fucked. Me? Blind? It's not me who's blind. Might as well pluck out my eyes as ask me not to see how everyone is selling out one by one. I can't stand the community's simple answer: We're here! We're queer! Put us on the front page of the *Gazette*!

Jesus, Rae says. You're hysterical.

A year or two in this oversimplified social strategy and your brain goes numb, Robin says, pointing to the couples dancing in the swirling light. Passivity sets in. Do you think one woman on that dance floor cares about sexual liberation? I hate our times, she says, drawing hard on each syllable.

Resistance exists, you think.

Rae crushes out her cigarette suddenly, scoffing, Smoking stinks. Robin thrusts her hands deep into the pockets of her trousers.

Rae says, Robin, this is Nora Flood. Nora, Robin.
Hello.

Robin looks at you and the lines around her eyes soften and slip. Then the clock strikes twelve.

Robin takes your hand and leads you to the centre of the dance floor. I do not want to be here, she says, then offers nothing more. She pulls you toward her, your bodies touching. You falter slightly, awkward and out of step: She waits for you. Her flesh is cool in your hand like a magnolia bud ripped from its branch in a pitching wind, the perfume her skin exhales the damp ground beneath that tree. Montreal becomes spring for an instant, for that moment in deepest December, for that moment in a smoky room within an abstract embrace. You think you should not look at her, for if you do you will become mere belly. Your appetite peaks.

You count the beats in a phrase, wanting the song to end. You can see Rae waving the bottle, beckoning you to come back.

Rae is one of my oldest friends, you offer to Robin as you move away from the dance floor. Rae's heavy glare terrifies you.

Not for long, is what Robin says.

It would be so easy. So easy to lie down in the shadows of the clock striking twelve. We're here! for this one hour only, the hour you first meet. The one and only hour self-contained in its own light.

Will you ever pick up a girl and take her home, promise her nothing, massage her feet, tell her she is beautiful and never see her naked again? Robin wants everything. She lacks nothing. She is unmanageable. She believes in her thoughts. She feels no shyness about her voice.

She needs you.

It is now ten in the morning, and she has finally gone to work. The two of you will not speak today. Don't ask her when next you see her, Do you love me? From now on, only ask questions the answers to which you are prepared to hear.

Is anyone there?

You walk on the mountain. Robin has asked you out on a second date and now she asks as you roll a snowball, Have you always been afraid of women?

You would have given anything to be able to tell her all the things of your life.

I'm afraid of lies, you say.

Robin stops walking and turns to you. The strong muscle of your heart clenches.

I promise you this, Nora: I will not lie.

All the light in the world and all its inky darkness will still seem to overwhelm me tomorrow. The sun will continue, but I will stand here at the window with my fists clenched, tense and strangely calm, transfixed. The sky beyond the sun will be a mass of black cloud. A third course of the storm will hit the city before noon.

I know I have made a dream out of imagination, out of intelligence. I must not blame Jefferson.

What did you do today, Nora? he asks each night when he comes home, the smells of the ranging outdoors clinging to the wool he wears.

I made this collage out of magazine scraps, Daddy. See? Sitting all afternoon, in the middle of the living room carpet with my leotard-clad legs spread wide as I could make them go, the sound of scissors cutting red construction paper like something I could carry away with me, torn glossy magazines everywhere. See? Everyone had to walk around me, Daddy.

He does not seem pleased. Did you tidy up and put your things away, Nora?

O, yes, Daddy. Will you look at my picture?

Very nice.

Jefferson: The holy provider, the mind we read. Some nights he does not come home until after I have gone to bed, and the next day he is invincible mind. He tells me about this world as if the world we are given were all there is.

What is the world, Jeff?

Water, mostly, you've got to learn to sink or swim. Swim to the banks. Dry out in the hot sun.

In which direction lie the midden flies, Daddy?

Do you always have to be so moribund, Nora? The world is what you make it. I believe that at certain times in a life, a person is held back by nothing at all. At certain times a person can do anything.

You look very alive, she says, her wild eyes feverish in the dark at the end of the bed, and then she goes into the bathroom and shuts the door.

How to respond to swift change in this tracing of

Robin's movements? Is she alive too? Is she trying to teach you a lesson? Punish you? Or is she as worried as you? Who can lay bare their hearts?

You go to the bathroom door. Are you crying in there, Robin? you ask.

Of course not, she slurs.

Anything wrong?

Her voice rises up. Nothing. What about you?

No, Robin. Not yet.

Well then, she says. I'll come out. We'll drink a toast. A toast to the end of the day.

The backyard in Port Credit is all of my childhood. Long and wooded with old maples and one tall black walnut. My younger cousins and I follow my sister Grace through the trees and over the narrow green lawn and grey driveway, the Merry Men to her Robin Hood, the wild horses to her cavalier, the wives and molls to her soldier. We three — the cousins and me — bruised and bloody as proofs of our devotion to the spirited Grace. She scares the shit out of us.

Remember when Maid Marian kissed you full on the lips, Grace?

No.

The adults call her leader of the pack. She organizes

the whole neighbourhood into teams with her rules and her punishments and threats. It is between us then as it is now.

Remember when you threw me off the top of the slide, Grace?

Yeah.

Remember how we used to hug naked in the bathtub?

We never did that, Nora.

Your oldest sister Jeannette spends most of her free time inside with her head in a book, tumbling among the words. You love reading just as much as Jeannette and see nothing perverse about it but your parents read Dr Spock and become mad about fresh air, trying to lure Jeannette out of doors with the promise of a peaches-and-cream complexion.

You see Jeannette exactly as she was, and she was yours. She develops a ritual of picnicking alone in your mother's rose garden, spread out on Grandmother Flood's old steamer carpet with a stack of books and a thermos of cold milk. You're quiet as a worm as you try to sneak up on her and share her spot in the sun. Get out of here, Nora. Go on, lose yourself! I love you but you're a pain in the ass. You wonder how she stands it

27

there in the garden, for your mother, in an effort to deter deer from nibbling her roses, has tied bars of Ivory soap throughout it, and the smell is overpowering.

Jeannette is top of her grade for five years in a row, and Grace and you do not even try to compete. She is tender, brilliant — a bright star in the schoolyard. And then — just before her sixteenth birthday. She has been reading, has stopped on her way home from debating club, has been standing still against the rough bark of a maple tree, oblivious to the flash and turn of spring traffic, her book held before her dark swooping eyes, enraptured by poetry's own sweet self. And then around the corner an old Chevy comes flying at random toward Jeannette and her tree.

When Grace and you return to the scene of the accident a few days after the funeral, you find a copy of Walt Whitman's *Leaves of Grass* soggy in the ditch, wrenched from Jeannette's hand.

There was a child went forth every day,
And the first object he look'd upon, that object he became,
And that object became part of him for the day or a certain
part of the day,
Or for many years or stretching cycle of years.

You don't speak of Jeannette in the years following her death. There is no compensation in touch for the lack of words between parents and children. Grace and you understand the rules: You are forbidden to discuss her. Put your toys away. Sink or swim.

Nothing will bring her back, Jeff tells you when he discovers you weeping among the hand-me-down clothes in your closet, a candle burning dangerously close to the soft falling cotton.

It's best to get on with living now, Nora. We only live once and if we are brave we live life the way we like and like it all the time we live it. Don't you think Jeannette would want you to be brave?

You don't know what Jeannette would want but you are sure you and she would lie together in the dark, telling each other over and over your own rendition of the story of the day she died. In each remembrance you will try to be less vulgar about what hurts. If this pleases Jeannette, you never know.

Let's talk, says spoilsport to optimist, three months into Robin's skin. You'll bolt. You will.

No I won't. I've given it up. I don't care about her other lovers. I want to learn how to love. I came from Toronto looking to love.

We'll see, stubborn girl.

Robin puts her tender mouth on yours. This takes the world by surprise.

Nothing is given to us, Nora, she says, her female body exposed.

Robin begins to teach you about silence. The tick of a second hand. A world turning. Systems hardening and cracking. Bone ground down beneath the skin. Crumbs tracked through a forest.

The unbearable mind, alone.

Robin has not come home. I set up my tripod in the bathroom. I make the bed. I take two aspirin, rinse my mouth. I phone Rae.

And then, abruptly, a small brown bird flies across this winter room.

I masturbate in the shower, feel clench of buttock and strain of thigh as I pinch my nipple and frenzy my hand against my pelvic bone. My blood swirls in the eddying waters. I am suddenly unable to stand, and slip down into the tub, the water coming at me from the shower nozzle in fierce drops. I think the only room in the world I need now is this room, this wet tiled place of glistening porcelain surfaces and the heavy unknowable body slumped against its own dreaded arousal. This is not agoraphobic thinking: I will want to walk the public thoroughfares again while also living this new, private experiment deep in the anxious folds of my heart and its terrible loneliness. Its madness is its secrecy, of course. I realize it is only me, a modern-day case, alone in the world.

Today I will remember yesterday.

In my masturbatory fantasy I am in an unknown office stairwell, my back against the wall. A man I have just met is before me on his knees, pants swirling around his ankles. His tongue unravels. I taste good to him. The androgynous mind might leap ahead one full century, might imagine a new woman, fierce and pigheaded in her bisexual faith, but I have no genius for that kind of leaping, and no available way to block the grievances that pour into my female mind once the rocking of my body subsides.

She has forsworn you.

Rae grinds out her cigarette in the ashtray before beckoning to the waiter, Encore. Do you want another? she asks you. You nod. Rae turns quickly, her fingers calling, Two more.

You have not seen each other since New Year's Eve. Rae is restless, edgy. She pulls another cigarette from her pack and pierces the filter with a needle she keeps laced in the lining of her jacket.

So how is it between you and Robin? she asks, her words spinning in the quick fall of extinguished match to floor. Are you in love? the word distorting in her grimace. Do you have a future? she questions, the sentence ugly.

Have you ever been with a woman, Rae?

Once, she says. Dreadful. Unmitigated anguish, violent. The beers come, and Rae pushes the total and tip into the waiting hand.

Women are so schooled in self-control, love between us is impossible, Rae says, sipping her beer.

I am standing still in the centre of a suffocating cone of heavy brocade drapery, suppressing a giggle, hiding from Jeannette. The year's sun and decomposing heat have been trapped in the weave of the weighted cloth and are now disturbed by my recent twirling, become a lively pillar of dry dust motes. It is narcotic.

Ready or not, you must be caught! Jeannette yells from the kitchen, her counting complete. Grace has inched her way into a crouch behind the rose-coloured chesterfield.

Nora, she hisses. Quit breathing so loud. I can hear you.

It's dusty in here, I whisper, slightly tipsy, my voice muffled.

Quiet!

I begin to count. Number of steps to the fridge, ten. Number of steps to the kitchen doorway, four. To the table in the hall, fifteen. Five more.

A red ball. A hairy comb. Myra's gold lamé clutch.

Deep quiet.

And then I hear Myra begin her descent, down from the large front bedroom where she has been sitting at her dressing table, flattered by its mirror's starlet lights, to our little game in the living room.

Mother, Jeannette trills as Myra comes into the centre of our game, now foundered. You look beautiful.

Grace sighs ever so slightly.

Mom, Jeannette continues. You look like a tropical fish. No. A mermaid. That fabric! Its threads are glinting! They're twinkling! Boy! Aquamarine. And gold!

Myra's wonderful perfume is filling the room.

Your father and I should be home by midnight, Myra says, ignoring Jeannette's gushing. There are hot dogs for supper, and ice cream in the freezer.

Jeannette listens.

And Nora can have her chocolate bunny if she gets ready for bed by eight.

Okay, Mom, Jeannette says.

And only one hour of television, no more.

Even me?

Even you.

Aww —

One hour. Why don't you take the girls to the park or something. A walk would do you good. You're starting to slouch.

Mom —

And don't forget your key if you do go out to the playground.

Mom —

And where are the girls, anyway?

Jeannette sighs. Nora is behind the curtains, she says. And Grace, I know you're there behind the couch.

Shit, Grace says, then gives an unexpected sneeze.

My giggles let loose.

Come out from there, snooks, Myra says to me.

I come out, and catch my breath, for she is beautiful in the fine dust falling through the light, just as Jeannette has said.

Mommy, I say, you are a picture.

Jefferson says he will take you to visit your great-aunt Muriel who lives on the edge of the city. Muriel, with her big house and her two efficient Chinamen and her two black Labrador retrievers and her sterling silver charm bracelet with its strange and compelling charms from the East; Muriel likes Jefferson awfully and seems rather fond of you. In particular, Muriel likes to go for a Sunday drive in her 1919 Morgan convertible, over to Halton Hills then down the back roads of Brant County, accompanied by the two of you. You are nine years old.

You sit in the back seat with your small hand holding on to your white felt beret, the wind rushing past your one exposed ear, unable to make out a single word flying back and forth between Jeff, who drives, and Muriel, beside him in the passenger seat, wildly gesticulating. The summer sun beats down, freckling your skin. You stop for a picnic lunch. Stilton cheese with its stinky blue veins, broken atop sesame crackers from China. Anjou pears with their green skin and white flesh, cut precisely in sixes. Everything spread out on a tartan steamer rug.

Jeff takes off his shoes and socks and rolls up his pant legs. His feet are stark with tendons, and very pale. He wiggles his toes and smiles at you. Then he strikes a match and smokes a cigarette filched from Muriel's fancy monogrammed case.

Not every child has such refined taste buds, Muriel says. I just adore watching Nora eat a pear.

You are allowed to ask questions on these picnics, questions forbidden most other times. You ask Muriel if she believes in God.

We are so impatient with the evil in the world, but it gives me comfort, Nora, to think that perhaps there is a design to it.

You persist.

What do *you* think, Daddy?

I think some little girls get away with murder away from their mothers on a Sunday picnic blanket in the country; so there must be a God.

You're getting away with murder, too, you know.

How's that? he asks.

That was Muriel's last cigarette.

O, how charming! Muriel cries. Nora, darling, you must try to show a little restraint. You will learn soon enough that everyone needs their little secrets.

Do they?

Yes. You can trust me on this. There isn't a soul alive who hasn't had to learn how to undress little white lies.

A blue jay swoops down from its branch in the oak tree above your head and hops toward you on the grass, so close you can make out the black necklace on its downy throat. You throw a sesame cracker to its feet. It pecks at the seeds in quick pitches, then takes the whole cracker into its beak and lifts up again into the tree.

Jeannette and I have our secrets, you tell Muriel.

Do you? Muriel asks. Do you talk to Jeannette sometimes, child?

When she comes to see me. But we don't talk. Like now. She's been standing over there by that statue of the little girl ever since we arrived.

For chrissakes, Nora, Jefferson shouts.

She is there, Daddy. Over there.

Jeannette is dead, he shouts again.

I know, Daddy. I know.

I am counting this day. The seconds until the aperture snaps. The number of steps between the studio and me. Counting to an old rhythm, a drumming that drowns out more subtle beats. I walk the winter streets, my head an anvil on which the aspirin works slowly, each count folding down into the next until I am no longer aware of it, indeed, until I forget that I feel anything. Or that anything at all is happening. The city has tipped, it pours itself into my emptiness, and I am cerulean blue.

I move into a one-and-a-half above a Portuguese bakery. The smell of bread is narcotic. I trample crumbs. Mice run the edges of my bed, cockroaches scale the high walls. I buy a secondhand light meter and a stovetop cappuccino maker. I collect unemployment for a little while, I think some thoughts and speak to no one. Myra's letters admonish me, Jeff's postscripts enrage me. I have lost something that every other girl seems to have found.

I wait for someone to speak to me. Wait in cheap cafés; wait in feverish lineups at repertory cinemas, my beret all wrong; wait for a stranger to say *je suis dans la lune* meaning I am the spoon she — the dish — wants to run away with.

I wait for the conversation that will restore my faith in something I never even knew I believed, a conversation with a stranger, a conversation that will require me to press into unexplored realms of my own real body and begin the excavation. I dream these conversations, these perfect narratives, and by day yearn for them as one yearns for the return of clean rose light through an evening window. But the city cares nothing for me. Cares nothing for my longing, does not think of me in any way.

I begin to wonder if survival means giving up waiting for a stranger to call me by name.

Fifty-five, fifty-six, fifty-seven. To the tall Québécoise approaching me on this narrow sidewalk, I look normal enough, except perhaps for my hair which is too short and my secondhand pants which are too loose and my gaze which is too punctured and my Nikon camera which seeks the darkest black and brightest white in this approaching storm. Anglophone, she will think. Not every passing woman looks away into deep space or out of living space into the superficial six square metres of front yard after front yard corralled by the wrought iron that is downtown Montreal. Some women catch each other's eyes here. But today I cannot bear to look her way.

I catch the scent of her as she passes, she has wrapped

herself in it, and now me. The perfume makes me nauseous. I feign a shoelace of my boot come untied so that I may stop, squat to the icy sidewalk and wait for the waves of nausea to pass. I turn my neck to watch her departing figure shifting obliquely in the snowflakes that have begun to fall. Her ass rides high above her confident stride. Who taught her to walk like that? Years of hiding in my hips, years of training and courses and being told how to do everything except how to keep panic out of my pelvis.

I am trying to get to the studio today only Myra is telling me to pull in my stomach and something is being said about hunger. If I lower my back and hips, let my pelvis widen, shorten, there is no mistaking unreal hungers then.

I am trying to get to the studio but I walk the streets, disconsolate, loosened in my flesh. I am trying to get to the studio but a pelvis tilts and knees lock in a desperate attempt to stand steady. A bitter storm approaches. I go over and over the same movement in this cold improvisation and I am trying for a way to move my body into this world.

But I am unable to do it, and I fall back, into myself.

Being a sex radical at this time is less a matter of what you do and more a matter of what you are willing to think, entertain, question.

Robin has underlined this. You two have been talking about living together for almost a year and you have begun to stumble over her things left lying about on the floor of the one-and-a-half. You pick up the book and continue to read where Robin has left off, waiting for her to return.

You are watching and not listening to Robin speak about something. You are thinking of kissing. You are superimposing your mouth over Robin's mouth and thinking about your lack of finesse in the kissing department. You are questioning jealousy, entertaining liberation. You are an old-fashioned girl, stiff with virtue. You are wondering if you should talk to Robin about this shortcoming. You are wondering if Robin —

You are watching the ten o'clock news on Robin's TV. You say to Robin that it seems the more television you watch, the more misinformed you are. The image, giddy American soldiers. Homesick, the voice-over says.

Robin puts her book down and watches you watching television. Nora, she says finally, I want to live together, don't you?

You turn in your chair. The image and Robin's voice-over focus and hold. Or so it seems.

I watch from the window as a half-dead cat drags itself uphill from the place on the road where it has been hit to the sloping sidewalk, and lies there, panting. I am caught like a fox in a steel-toothed trap.

Chew off your own leg? Stay? Or go?

Does Robin think like this?

I stand at the window, and the cat expires while I languish in this tedious preoccupation between screech and moan. Stay? Or go? I swing between, flooded by grief. I do not want to agree with the wounding thought now broken out once again from its own scar tissue: She cannot love you. This wound is screaming, hurling itself against iron rails, concrete sidewalks, the endless flesh of Jeannette.

Is there no one at all to blame for what I now suffer, having willingly sacrificed my tenderness, my capacity to love? I know how to cradle a dying cat in my arms, yet I did nothing.

Her breath on your skin is impossibly tender and sad.

I want you, Robin says.

Her dark eyes, the way her black hair rides away from her forehead, her impenetrable gaze, her boyish body, the way her white cotton undershirt drapes across the erect nipples of her soft apple breasts; the bite of her, her coltish hips; the descent of her arousal; her serenity: You want her.

Wait here, you say.

In the bathroom you refuse the mirror, look above it as you wash your cunt and your hands and dry them on the thin green towel. You feel the arrival of shame like a sudden rash across your belly. Above the sink there is a window that opens into a narrow vertical shaft. You open it. Distant voices call out to one another, dimly, *Bonne Année, bonne nuit*. It is snowing, a slow light fall. Thick snowflakes drift in through the open window and land on your naked shoulder. You watch the crystals melt into tiny pools.

Nora.

She is at the bathroom door.

Nora, she says again.

You turn and give her your best smile, then cross your hands over your own soft breasts. She enters the room, kneels before you and takes your quickening vulva in her wet mouth. Your knees buckle and you pitch forward, grab her stormy head, and come.

You lie on the bed, naked, sober, sobbing, She's gone, She's gone, I'm my own body now. You do this because Robin has told you she has made love to another woman, and because she informs you that she is like this. You think she means you can either get used to your own sobbing or you can move out.

You have always known that Robin is Like This. That first morning when you returned from the bakery with milk and croissants, steamy with the new year's wet chill, she told you she was like this. You understood her, and you both laughed, Robin's long and elegant neck thrown back.

You have had conversations about this. You have dreamed and drifted in endless flesh, flesh which turns to need, a million dreams and memories unlocked in your molecular spaces, your dreaded body.

You moved in together. You moved into each other. You picnicked between sheets, between thighs. Your bodies in infinity became something you said you could bear. She continued to go her way and you went yours in the ways of work. But when it comes to your own circle, you don't always know exactly where it starts and where it ends. You find yourself unable to move, caught in an odious counting that gradually, day by day, draws you into its sterile heart. You stop going outside and start putting numbers on things to keep out the emptiness. You have your lover lines well stocked. You

drink from each other every day. And then one day she
wants to stop you from pouring all your self into her
one glass.

What could change her now, now that she has left
you in this one small room and moved out into the
lonely vastness of the world?

Grace has the smile of a hyena among the company of
our family. After Jeannette dies, she and I spend weekends
at our grandmother Alice's house in Toronto's east end.
After our grandfather dies of emphysema, the weekends
cause a kind of emotional suffocation in Grace and she
refuses to go. I keep on, hatching my own private suffering
that goes on and on, measured into my weekdays in Port
Credit, into my dreams, into the closet that shields me
from Jeff's alien words. My single bright candle.

We sit at Alice's kitchen table. Do you miss Jeannette?
Alice asks as we slurp ice cream from a cool spoon.

Sometimes, Grandma.

It's all right to cry if you do.

Is it?

O, darling child, she laughs, her linen napkin loosen-
ing from beneath her chin and drifting to the floor. I
stoop to pick it up for her, trying to compose my hidden
self as Jeff has taught me to do. Think of a stone, he would

say, think of an octopus shifting its shape and colour to confuse its predators, and I suddenly realize that a stone is bowling through the dark recesses of my heart and its droning blood. I look up, my gaze coming to rest where the flesh of Alice's loose thigh folds between garter and silk stocking. An unfamiliar voice speaks in my head.

The wish to be good is the wish to be destroyed.

I straighten up immediately.

You are pulling the lens, but the light will not converge over her drenched form. Glorious. She lies naked against a large warm flagstone, roused from a daydream above a luminous lake. The skin of her belly slides over her protruding hip. She watches you as you adjust your aperture, the whites of her eyes like wet abalone.

You scan the surface of her flesh, you order the lines of her waking beauty, you feel your way around the boundaries of this performance of hers and yours, the one so mysterious and new, the other so bent on speculation.

Stay with me, she says suddenly, sitting up, cupping her palm over her pubis, shy, awkward, folding her other arm across her breasts, hanging her head. Though there is something undoubtably wrong with me, Nora, please. Don't leave me.

This day one hour in Paradise.

When my father announces his sudden decision to move us to Vancouver, I ask to spend the next weekend with Alice. As she tucks me into my small bed, I tell her my plan: I won't be going to Vancouver with the family, I will come to live with her. Together we will eat her homemade macaroni and cheese, her chocolate pudding from scratch, her stovetop mayonnaise. She can count on me. I will never leave her.

Your father has been unhappy at his job, Nora.

He's a liar and a cheat, I say, not comprehending. I wish aloud that Jeff were dead. I cry in her arms, and fickle though I am Alice knows how to lead me through that dark night.

The mental effect of virus pneumonia makes it difficult to put one's foot down: One can hardly stand up. Foiled by a temperature of 103 degrees Fahrenheit, and by a father who pronounces the drive across Canada good for what ails us all, and by a mother who turns her back to tend her garden, even into twilight, I watch, resigned, from a wooden lounge chair beneath the magnolia tree while my cousins from Etobicoke come for one last time to pound over the lawn, pulling Grace's chariot. We drink cherry Freshie and smile gigantic smiles made more huge by our red moustaches and then Grace picks up the end of my chair and drags me around the yard while Myra hollers from the porch and the cousins shriek with a confused hysterical glee. Later, as Grace and I roll around on the lawn with the cat, and the cousins play jumpsies on the driveway, Myra comes out to the garden to give her roses one last long look. She bends down to her favourite Jens Munk, clutching its stem, and I watch as she straightens quickly, thrusting her finger into her downturned, tightened mouth, and sucks on the blood that jumps up out of the skin. It is said within the rose's memory the gardener is never forgotten. Myra turns, and goes back into the house.

Jeff comes home at five to congratulate Myra on her organizational skills, on the untroubled transition from the tidy daily living which has been our ordinary lives to the tidy, well-packed car which will be our home for the five-day drive across Canada, cat and maps at our feet. He finds me lolling in the stairwell, mounting an impossible idea as my hold on the fact of our departure plummets, and he puts his hand to my feverish head. He smells of mown grass, of shit and stale cigarettes.

Leave whatever it is you are doing here and join the family, he commands.

My aunt Joan brings cold chicken for supper which

we eat with our fingers because the cutlery and plates are long gone in the moving van. Jeff calls us hooligans, and sits in a makeshift chair he constructs out of boxes, one leg tossed over the other, eyes focused on some invisibility in a concentrated distance. Grace excuses herself to go to the bathroom and I think she runs across the school-yard to the place on the road where Jeannette was hit.

Where have you been? Myra asks when Grace comes back to the living room where we sit cross-legged on the floor.

Toilet.

What took you so long?

Grace draws a long slow breath before looking up through her bangs, and she says, Stuck on a rock, and all the adults laugh.

Myra takes one last look around the house, closing cupboard doors and sucking back about sixteen ounces from the cold water tap. Then Jeff lifts me up into his strong arms and carries me out to the drive, we Floods get into the Pontiac and drive away.

You begin to teach her about light and shadow, about gaseous activity in the brain, about swift almost impercep-tible openings and closings of a shutter, how to remove unnecessary weight in a picture, in a bed. You draw her a home and point to her room. You give her a key to a door. You stand on the other side.

Night. July. Why did Jeff want to leave Port Credit under stars? I wondered. Both Jeff and Myra were born in Ontario. It was our home. The Don Valley Parkway and Gardiner Expressway now linked us to thousands of hopeful others.

Why then were we sneaking out of town like thieves?

I ask him. Many times. And he gives the same questionable answers about time and money and change. Jeff goes on to remind me of the spectacular sunrise we watched from a roadside stop outside Blind River. I am left helplessly sleeping in the Pontiac with the cat at my feet while Myra, Jeff and Grace admire the morning sky and wolf down johnnycakes and maple syrup at an inn near Thessalon.

Leaving our house at night makes me crazy with a second grief for Jeannette and more hostile toward Jeff than ever before. Riding in the back seat of that silent night with my arms around my aching chest, feeling murderous, ready to explode at the mean misfortunes of my eleven years, I try to quiet myself by counting — other cars on the highway, orange windows of distant farmhouses, black shapes I take for owls flashing by the car — as if the only thinking I can trust myself to do is thinking in numbers, counting in the cadence of an abandoned child rocking herself into someone's elaborate company.

O, Jeannette. O, Toronto. These are the nights of my terrible losing, the girl, her real body and silhouette shadow moving across the Canadian landscape, a million shining dreams and hopes billowing out behind her in dark unassuming time.

What do you want to do each time she leaves you alone at home while she prowls? What do you want to do? Is what you want to do anything like what you do?

She is not leaving you. She wants you, she says.

What do you do?

You drink two glasses, one hundred bottles, of wine, you pace the circumference of one hundred small rooms, you cry for half an hour, you drink another glass of wine, you make yourself something to eat and don't eat it, you vacuum, you fall into bed and cry for another year.

The wind gives an occasional knock on the window. The hours roar. Years measure the weight of your briefest motion. You crave her arms around you and curse her name. This is what you do. And while you do these things you imagine her, prowling the dark streets, sacrificed to the contingencies of other women's flesh beneath the veils of night. And all the while you do these things you talk out loud, you say, This is what you have, you say this out loud over and over, you say, You must count the time spent with Robin in minutes and hours, not days and years.

Nothing is given to you, you say.

You have made many starts to photographs you can't finish because your eye leads you to a place where the next inevitability is Robin drunkenly fisting another woman, them all naked and sweaty and bright, coming up laughing and never thinking of you. The stories cannot be named when the film goes on so blankly.

You imagine instead a turning rope as it thuds on thick carpet, the dull sound bouncing off walls. Jute hairs catch in the red carpet's weave. You try to imagine a woman called Nora jumping alone in the dark. One hand, mind-forged, stretches to a lover gone away into the night. The other holds a camera.

You picture this:
When Nora first moved to Montreal, she lived in a tiny one-and-a-half above a Portuguese bakery. Graffiti on the side of the building read: *Dehors méchant*. Her upstairs neighbour translated.

It meens de snot in your face.

Nora met Robin at a New Year's Eve dance. Robin was sitting with Rae on the side stairway, smoking and sharing a bottle of cheap wine. Rae waved Nora over. They looked at each other. The clock struck twelve.

The rope continues to turn against carpet, the woman continues to jump. Nothing rests.

Robin kisses then stops. Hot fire runs from forehead to chest, singeing tiny hairs. She drops a woman to the floor.

She goes to a window and presses her fingertips to the peeling paint, tearing it from the wall. A woman goes up behind her and presses her breasts into Robin's back. Robin spins and slaps her. The woman falls to the floor.

The energy fails. Robin looks down on an upturned face and has no thought, no initiative, nothing to follow. They stand like that for a long time. Both want to stop looking at the other but neither can turn her head away.

The rope begins to catch sparks. A long way off, someone shouts, Fire.

A woman moves to her knees. Is her tongue hanging out? Are her moving fleshy parts bulging? Robin gets down beside her. She strokes the bone above breast, moving the flat of her hand over the ridge, slowly down, further down, over soft belly and Venus mons, in.

Freeze. She promised Nora she would be safe. There are gloves somewhere. Will she? Her real body with its heat and wet and breath, what is it asking for?

She could snap her. Her mind white, mad to play her

body, mad to wet her hand, mad to taste.

Nora looks at but no longer sees the tiny rope hairs catching in the carpet, the tiny flames scampering along its length. Now she lifts up her head, now the rope ends are dropped, now ice is hurled splitting into a winter night, she can make out the sky through the cracked moon. Stars have weight in this moment without ground. She covers her eyes with her cold hands.

What happens? You cannot take this picture. Hold steady, focus, crack wide open, resist the hand that holds you down.

O, you have hated her. You have thought you could not go on and you have gone on, desiring some first thought or certain image while your body sits at a table on a chair before a window looking out. Red is the colour of your landscape, rope and hangman's knots its texture. These cannot save you. Inside keeps turning while outside marks the distance. You are counting moons before breaking sky in two and mounting next sky, changing shape, growing old, a circular energy returning from sky, the personality trapped in its timed existence while Jeannette stands watch.

Witnessing how deeply sprung is the hate you hold toward the ineffable hurts most of all. In these minutes, describing what is not yet known, only there, there,

waiting to become colour, texture, ground, that is first-
born out of immediate ripping pain. You cry in your bed
in the darkest hour, alone, your mind on fire, your
meaty body certain of its boundaries, and your solar
plexus sure of its terror, its holy ground.

At first you see the light and then you cannot face the
light because the earth begins to roll and you are bolus
in a snake and then you're helpless. First you read the
words and then the letters start to fall and you are
fainting at the door the awful blood begins to heat and
you are seeking. First you say you can't and then the
door frame moves through you and the blood is very
hot and you are taking that first step so grotesque you
do not recognize your youth is getting thin and the
aperture is threatening how the skin begins to falter
and you take another step and someone howls and it is
you. First your hip descends a thickening nipple seeks
reflection and you don't know how to place it though
the face looks quite familiar but a face you've shied away
from photographs the hideous mocking you're so pitiful
while shrinking you've not learned too much about it
and the copulating sky unfurls you feel the push deep in
you and the leaving is the trying rare as rosebud innova-
tion and there's shrieking in the woodwork and a door is

blasted open and a hand is very shaky and you take a step towards her but there is no floor beneath you no device for strangulation and the choosing is beside you now what's vital is a chorus and they're laughing very loudly you know Nothing you know Nothing so repressed. Look at them with horror then capitulate in terror experiment with angel voices it's the hands inside the mocking it's the family repression and it's licking your subversion and your cunt can't get much higher and you're burning as you waver while the stone is fading from them and the turning burns inside you all its rope hairs iridescent as the words collapse around you Nothing there. First you step toward her her existence is the referent you're body making motion you're the choice the resurrection the idea and its body coming wet and coming through you her wide gift is there to serve you she is like some holy water she is ready at your service you can feel disintegration you can feel exhilaration you forego the forest crumbs bleeding maps and neon markers you are leaving you are leaving in a body all undone. Cast your eyes in water rosy water porcelain and the light is now before you and you're naked in your thinking but your body wants to carry yes you're bolus yes you're moving yes you're choosing yes you're trying O you're trying there is no way that it's done no way it's done.

꒚

Robin suggests a game you two can play on an early spring walk through the city. You will blindfold me then lead me along, she says. The challenge will be the slushy curbs, of course, but we can wear gum boots, do you have a pair?

You do not refuse her.

You hold her warm hand and as you walk together in the sun past strolling couples on the Main and lovers seated over steaming bowls in cafés on St-Denis, you describe Montreal to her, the city that will always be more hers than yours. I was born here, she tells you, my father is a surgeon. My mother died when I was three.

Where is your father now? you ask carefully.

I have lost track of him, she says. I have not seen him in ten years.

You take her to the old city and as you begin to describe the possible ways she might negotiate the cobblestone in her clumsy boots, she stops you.

I am beast turning human, she says, *à cause de toi*.

There is considerable resistance to any change in the fairy tale; all right to lose sight of the king and queen, and Prince Charming is not the answer. The emperor is as naked as a jay bird, but woe to the rebel who tries to assert ruthless ambition in Snow White, or lets Bilbo Baggins wander out onto a killing field. The happily-ever-after crowd goes really batty, reports the rebel to the crown, and off with her head.

Myra, can you please describe to me the face of your god?

Vancouver. I am sixteen and counting the days. Myra and Jeff are not amused by my discovery of: liquor, late nights, their powerlessness. Top of their list of complaints is my acquaintance with Donny Foden, immaculate and effervescent faggot, cape-flinging long-haired poet of False Creek, designer of brilliant macramé wall hangings commissioned by rich folk up the mountainside, and reader of impenetrable poems at Theodora's Café on evenings when the cold drives him out of his warehouse home. What words, Nora? I meet him after one of his readings; shy, but he smiles encouragement. He talks and I listen, stupefied. Then he invites me for a drink.

I'm only sixteen.

O, sweet boy. Sixteen, schmixteen, he laughs. You've got to give up believing in time.

I'm not a boy, Mr. Foden, I say.

He takes a step toward me, sniffing.

Ah, so it is, he says.

Donny loves wine, and drinks a daily bottle. He says I simply must accompany him and his entourage to a gay disco in the west end where Sylvester is spinning on the turntable, where lithe and hairless boys feel mighty real on the dance floor as their hands briefly pass over thin rubbed blue jeans bulging white in the crotch. Donny tells me that my face has amazing composition. He is thirty years old, and the first human being to suggest that while I am busy counting my stars I am lying in a gutter. I don't yet know he is quoting. He gives me hope.

See that boy over there, Nora?

I look in the right direction.

I'm betting on tonight's entanglement, he tells me.

O, I don't know — I begin.

Not with you, silly darling. He deplores beauty. No, I mean with me.

My life divides between English class and Donny, between poetry and wine. With the girls at school I am sullen, tongue-tied, eager to flee the front steps where they smoke and gossip and jostle. Myra says my heart is in Ontario, in Alice's kitchen and in the backyard of our house in Port Credit. Jeff says I have to come out of my shell. He says, Stop moping around, hiding behind your books. He is one to talk. Once he was a wonder to me, slamming angrily into the house with the scent of the outdoors lingering on his clothing. What did you do today, Nora? Now his arrival home from work is a theme in two variations: After kissing Myra, he falls into his chair with his evening paper, holding the pages wide, one leg crossed over the other, ankle-to-knee, showing dry skin between pant and sock, and for all we know he is catatonic behind the headlines. Or: He is away in Toronto on business, and returns strangely meek, defeated.

Donny says I have to give up living dead in my closet with my candle and diary, get a fresh haircut, take steps two at a time to strengthen flabby-tending thighs, and forget about my family who are, he says, a tedious pack of people without the remotest knowledge of how to live. He says the only thing that really matters is a girl's strong chin, and with my profile — the left side preferable to the right — I never need worry about being left out of society. Uncertain about inclusion, still I am grateful for Donny's attention.

I wonder why you love me, I ask one innocent day.

Honey, you are my blue flag, my iris prismatica. You are my Marianne Moore, my Edna St. Vincent Millay. If only I were the marrying kind.

You're gay, Donny.

Alas.

Rae orders another beer for herself.

You want one? she asks.

No. I think I'm going to get moving now.

We sit together silently for another half hour.

How many years have you been with Robin? Rae finally asks as we continue to watch Robin move around the bar, from person to person, from drink to drink.

Four years now, I tell her.

How many of those years did you go out looking for her, trying to bring her home?

She always manages to come home, Rae.

Rae says nothing.

I get up to leave, drop my money on the table knowing that Robin will return to me at night's end, me, the one who remains; and I walk home, glad that the walk will soon be over.

Another interminable night dreaming of binding our hearts together, like a nest in the flickering darkness.

Donny's style of dress makes him completely unavailable to Jeff and Myra who say he is perverse and consider his flamboyance my ticket to hell. Why can't you hang around with people your own age? they cry as I prepare to meet Donny at Theodora's. What is he hiding behind that mass of auburn hair? beneath that black cape? they beg.

You are not to see Donny any more, Jeff tells me one morning after hearing me sneak into my bedroom only hours before. We are sitting together at the kitchen table: Grace and Myra are upstairs getting ready for church. I no longer go with them: I am reading John Donne.

Why not? I ask, looking up from my egg.

No discussion, he concludes, dumping his plate and cup into the sink before wiping his hands on a Bless This Kitchen tea towel. Behind his back I count the seconds until he is out of the room.

When I relay the new conditions of my life to Donny, he takes another sip of his wine before explaining, Where's a man who could ease your heart like a good book? He sighs. That father of yours. A complete stranger to himself.

All these doors slamming. He sighs again. Your parents are only willing to see one side of the coin. There is a dark and terrible side, Nora, marvellous yes and horrible. Mascara is great but it can smear. Think of wine! The words practically pour out. They're afraid you'll become a dyke, he concludes.

What's that?

O, darling, what can I tell you? You are going to have to lie.

Robin's deep voice undulates as the flies drowse, an American goldfinch overhead catches your eye. You are taking a walk in the park and she is holding your hand as you play this familiar game: She walks blindfolded, you are her guide. With every step, you both become slightly less stable. You think she is learning to walk, delaying with each step the fall she fears. You assess the risks, one step at a time. You will not tell her what you are thinking. The landscape is drowning in pink. The future is a blaring horn.

You tell her this is where the road begins, this is where it ends, a slight incline here now a change in ground now sand now wet grass, and you think, Her world is that which I describe. What if she were always blind? What if she were unable ever again to see another woman's beauty? The unreliable idea becomes unbearable.

You want to raise your voice, praise marigolds' gold, the rosy light behind the maple keys, but to do so is to offer more love than you will ever receive. You see this now. Will it be so, now and forever, between the two of you? Every sense in your body doubles. She tells you about a poem she read in the *New Yorker* then interrupts herself to comment on the sound of the cicadas, Did you know it is only the males who chirp? They rub their mirrors to get attention.

She will never accept your destiny; only her own.

If you can discern a pattern in a bit of music, you can easily begin to move to the beat. The rise and fall, energy-versus-gravity sweep is deeply embedded in every move we make. This I am beginning to understand from the dope and the wine I have, from time to time, begun to overindulge in. I have discovered the drunken sensation of thighs as heavy as lead, of muscle collapsing. As I sit across from Donny with the sun pouring down on my face and Joni Mitchell on the tapedeck singing All I Want, a thousand adjustments are all that keep me from falling into a box and closing the lid. You are going to have to lie. I watch as Donny scoops his long thin hair away from his neck, hear the twitch of static on his black wool cape.

He is all for hiding things, just as Myra and Jeff suspected. I push back from the table and excuse myself.

I'll be right back, Donny.

In the washroom cubicle, something begins to creep over me. The skin on my face bulges, my head begins to roll. Something in my middle pulls everything to it.

Suddenly there is a knock at the cubicle, and a deep contralto voice says, Nora Flood, open this door immediately. I can see a pair of black pumps, like the ones Alice wears, shifting restlessly below the hem of a navy gaberdine coat. The shinbone is sharp as a blade, making the beige stockings shimmer in a dark vertical line. I straighten up, lifting my legs off the floor, my spine extending, arms clutching knees to my pounding chest.

Again the voice demands that I open the door.

No, I squeak. I'm not finished.

You listen to me, child, the stranger says. Donny is an old pansy who just wants you around for the sake of his ego. He's a dreadful bugger. Always quoting Oscar Wilde and Dorothy Parker. My god. They are all dreadful buggers, Jean Genets in love with the smell of their own farts. And I tell you, I didn't ever anticipate finding you weeping over an old pansy in a toilet somewhere. Now come out here, Nora, right now.

I lean forward and draw back the lock. The door sighs open an inch before an old wrinkled hand thrusts it, banging, against the cubicle wall. There you are, the old woman says. Well, let me take a look at you.

Her mouth is the first thing I notice. It purses rhythmically as she eyes me head to toe. The lower lip protrudes beyond the thin upper lip, the ends competing with the deep lines running from nose to neck, everything in constant adjustment. Her false teeth are badly fitted. She leans heavily on an elegant walking stick and seems a little out of breath. After a moment of intense gazing, she says, Normally we are all incapable of doing great and wonderful things, but it is my opinion that when we do manage a bit of greatness, we are not even ourselves but someone else.

Who? I ask, looking again at her heavy shoes, thinking again of Alice, wondering if I bolted past her would I knock her over.

She continues as if I had not spoken. When I was finished with you, I thought, my god, there's a survivor. She'll never speak again, of course, but she'll grow old knowing both privacy and poetry. If I'd foreseen this ill-gotten tendency in you I might never have written *Nightwood*. She says all this with obvious displeasure in me, and quite inexplicably I feel the need to impress upon this stranger the facts of my own weeping.

I only hoped — I begin, but she cuts me off with a sudden burst of kindness.

O, little tenderfoot, the tenet I have lived by is truth

at all costs. Critics say it was autobiographical, but I am not a lesbian. I simply adored her. One tells one's own story to beat off melancholy, that's all. Don't think I don't suffer, sweetie. And to answer your question, let the critics cast the first wretched lie.

And then she turns and walks slowly out of the women's washroom, her dark cane pressed roughly against the shining tiled floor.

I stumble to the mirror, searching in my reflection for anything familiar, seeing Alice's puffy feet as if projected onto a film screen, stuffed into too-tight shoes, her stockings thick, her legs like winter trunks beneath the table where I bend to retrieve a fallen linen napkin damp at its edges.

When I get back to the table, Donny is scribbling a poem onto his wine-spotted serviette, his inky words circling around the spills.

An old woman in the washroom called me tenderly by name, I say, quietly, realizing I am no longer depressed. Donny is too taken with his poem to notice me.

I said I just saw — a ghost.

Did you, darling? Do we have ghosts in British Columbia?

I dig around in my knapsack for a pen. On my own scrap paper I write: Manage a bit of greatness, uncertain of the hand that holds the pen, of the shoulder that gathers the knapsack to it, of the mouth that kisses

Donny's upturned distracted cheek goodbye. Bursting with the possibility of happiness. A stranger has called me by name.

Robin says, Come on, Nora. This is the first great lie. It has nothing to do with us, nothing to do with two women together. Let's at least be honest, for god's sake. I demand that you see this truth: We are all like this.

You're hurting me.

There is no place to run, Nora. No safe place. Things hurt. You gotta get tough. And death waits at the end to hurt us the most, it takes our last comforts and hurls them in our face.

If death intends to hurl something in my face, so be it. But you? Let go of me.

You put your eye to the lens, and there you must find consolation, however brief. Look to the light. Look to the shadow. Look to the natural divide between the father who is and the father who moves in secret, the mother who waves while wearing a frown. Look to the sister who hovers on the forsaken path, who yearns for your spirit to fill her own emptiness. Take my picture, she cries.

Put your eye to the lens. Adjust the aperture. Determine the shutter speed. Account for discrepancies in weight and tone. You are unknowable.

Take the picture. Steal the light. This moment will never finish.

Was Donny an artist? Or a vacuous, superficial quoter of Oscar Wilde? Did he invent or repeat?

O, sweet boy, he tells me, you're so gorgeous. So young and full of energy. No one's going to toss you out of bed for wearing glasses. If only I had your nerve.

O, yeah, right. *Nerve.*

Donny encourages me to peel away layers of my careful heart, to pay attention to the storms in my gut, to live in the words washing over me. Sometimes he turns and asks, What words now? and whichever ones are there I say aloud.

Sing!

Empty boats!

Once, flying through Stanley Park on rollerskates, Donny yells, What words? and I shout, Jeannette! I see her, crossing a field: She has Jeff's gait. She is heading toward this body of mine now bursting open.

I can't go on, Donny. Everything inside me has changed.

O, honey, come on. Don't be maudlin. I've lost my emotions altogether!

People pass us on the sidewalk but I am somewhere between the sidewalk and the mouth of a dark river. I am pressing one hand hard against my belly, can feel its roiling cords. Jeannette holds my other small hand in hers. She leans in to kiss my soft lips. In the far distance, Donny's golden earring blinks in the sun.

What words? he whispers.

Baby, I say, staring in front of me. The ocean groans beneath its boats. I force my eyes shut.

When I open them again, Donny is gazing out into the waves.

Donny, I have no women friends. Where are the women?

They're around the corner in a sandbox crying over spilled milk.

Be serious. Don't you know some women who would be delighted to meet a mostly sober sixteen-year-old?

Sure. Thelma.

Who's Thelma?

A photographer. I met her one night. Under a bridge.

Under a bridge? You're making her up.

No, I'm not, she's very real, darling, I'm afraid. Listen, you come round next Friday evening, you can meet her. You want to meet a woman, I have a woman. Simple.

Will I like her?

O, probably not. Nobody really knows Thelma.

Well, will she like me?

I promise she will fall madly in love with you but you will break her heart.

Thelma goes to school at the University of British Columbia. She studies criminology, thinks she might apply for a Rhodes Scholarship when she finishes her Bachelor's. She is nineteen years old and has a giant intellect. She tells me all this in a bored, offhand way as we sit together in Donny's tiny room, sipping Spanish wine and smoking mentholated cigarettes. Donny rolls a joint.

Thelma says she wants to be a lawyer, but what she already is is a fabulous photographer, he tells me between rapid-fire tokes. That is how we met. She takes pictures at night. Only at night.

Really? How weird!

Weird? Why, weird?

Well, of course you can see it's a bird you're photographing, for example, but how can you see what colour it is? or what kind of bird?

I'm not searching for birds at night, she says with disdain.

I don't answer.

You need me to see? she says finally. All right. I can

74

see everything in the flash, Nora.

Yes. But by then it's too late, isn't it? I mean, by then the picture is already taken, no?

Photography isn't like that: That's someone's pretty idea of photography. And night isn't like that either. People think night has to resist any border of light. People think night is a lesser day. But really, night simply shows up day for what it lacks. Night haunts day. That's why people cheer a full solar eclipse. It's the one time night really gets inside.

Lucky you have a flash attachment, is all I say.

Why do sisters fight? Do we spot some resemblance in the other that we would rather not see, wanting to cling to the notion of our absolute separateness and difference? Is her face before us proof that the history we are trying to rewrite cannot be separated from what we feel, looking at her? How many sisters tally disappointments like stitches in cloth? the passage of losses left in the flesh? a vast cross-hatched landscape, every pain and joy discernible in every shade, the grid of our parallel lives? Maybe we learn too well the boundaries of our fathers' ground, their definitions and demarcations — if you are brave you will live life the way you like and like it all the time you live — forgetting how we are bound together in bodies rolling around beyond the man's lawn.

If we learn our rules through the men who raise us, can we only evolve by rejection of all that lovely round rolling in the grass?

And what about Myra? Why lie with me, mouth open, waiting for the magnolia petals to fall, if the point of the lesson was patience only?

Grace always could lie better than me. There has been a long silence between us; one of her best deceptions. Why does she not call or write? I tell Robin I can hear anything Grace wants to tell me, but when the light slices through Robin's eye, I remember who I am. The correct approach, I realize later, is to consider the finite situation first.

Remember how we used to hug naked after a bath, Grace?

We never did that, Nora.

I have hung a large sheet of silver foil on the east wall of the studio. The air is melon-coloured in the late September afternoon, sunlight flooding through the west window above St-Laurent. Robin is my rosy model reflected and repeated in the foil's creases. We have been seeing each other for nine months.

Do you think Manet got a hard-on when he was

painting his models? she asks.

Probably. All those pinks and blushes. Those violets. But I think he was polite about it.

Jeannette is here, reading Emily Dickinson on a stool in the corner. She has been coming around somewhat frequently since I started my affair with Robin. She likes to watch me set the studio lights. She says the way a shadow crosses a room tells everything about immortality.

She says, Robin is very beautiful. She has a sort of fluid blue moving beneath her skin.

How old were you when you first started to think about sex? I ask.

Robin says, Six or seven. I had a babysitter, Laura. She used to bounce me on her knee while she read Dr Seuss out loud. Somehow she is all mixed up with that bouncing and jiggling, that smear of pink on the snow that the Cat got rid of, and those green eggs.

Jeannette says, Just a week before I was killed I dreamt that Jefferson and I were lovers. We made love in Mom and Dad's bed.

Jesus. Really?

Robin smiles. Yeah. Maybe if I'm good you'll wear a top hat for me one day? Or we could do it in a house with a mouse?

We're doing that already, I say, distracted, lifting my head from the camera, turning to Jeannette, my eyebrows raised.

No. We're doing it in a one-and-a-half with a mouse.

It was a dream, Nora. A dream celebrating Jeff's allure.

Does it disgust you?

Robin says, I love you.

I'm glad for it, Jeannette says. Remember how handsome he was? Remember how great it felt to hold his big hand?

He's dying now, I tell Jeannette.

I know. You should take Robin to meet them before he does.

What? Did you lay a mousetrap?

I don't have any money.

My love, a trap costs less than a bagel in this city.

What did you say?

I said a mousetrap —

No. Before that.

Robin rattles the foil like thunder.

I have been commissioned to take photos on the Main, to document its degeneration, its foreclosures. When I am finished, the work will be shown. Nothing will change.

After my move to Montreal, I think it might improve things if I were to tell Jeff and Grace that I am a dyke. Myra has encouraged it. She writes to say that during family discussions about the United Church decision to ordain homosexuals, Jeff has shown something Myra feels bad denying. It is the only time I have felt grateful for the church.

Myra has insisted on this secret for years, and this insistence has made me want to get into her, trowel in hand. When I was six, Jeannette told me that if I dug deep enough in Myra's garden, I would get to China. I thought she'd meant the country.

So many things I never wanted to know about the place inside a soul where porcelain grows.

Myra is wrong about Grace. She calls, however, the day she gets my letter. Doesn't say much. Mostly talks about Jeff's health. Bone cancer. Finally she says that nothing matters so long as I still take breath, and hangs up. The echo of her voice stays with me that day, circles around me like a loose thread. I repeat Grace's words verbatim to Rae who cocks her head to the side, lifts her eyebrows and says, Well Christ! what more could you want? At least she didn't tell you that you were damned to burn in eternal hellfire.

Rae, who can't resist eating hearts whole.

Sometimes I want to tell Grace of the moments along Robin's skin, the superb nights, the glory of gravity.

I want to tell her how hardly an evening goes by that I don't look into the sky observing how we are moving around on a spinning globe in unknowable space, and how those observations lead me to think about how long it has been, this You desiring a future. I want her to dare me like when we were small, I want the picture of us sitting side by side in the ragweed near the spot where Jeannette was hit, our two heads bent, our eyes spilling on Walt Whitman's words:

The sense of what is real
the thought if after all it should prove unreal.

Is there only so much truth, really, and the rest we manufacture? Is real truth-telling imperceptible, the lightest gossamer thread woven through our words?

Grace, remember when Jeff and Myra let us drink wine and eat sourdough bread with Stilton cheese during our picnic by the ocean? How Jeff and Myra waltzed in the waves?

You're out of your mind, Nora.

Grace, are you tired of going back and forth to Vancouver to see Jeff?

I don't do it for me, Nora.

Grace, what does Jeff talk about? Does he talk about dying? Does he talk about his body? Has he mentioned any secrets? Does he talk at all? Of Jeannette? O, Grace, does he talk about me?

Still hoping, Nora? After all these years? You really are something else.

Grace, I want to know, does Jeff have long now?

The nurses say he'll be home by Friday, but I don't think he'll ever see home again.

Grace, I'm afraid Jeff will be dead before I get there.

The phone line issues a slight hiss.

Take your time, Nora. He won't know you now.

What, really, is the point of all this questioning? Is it sensible? Is it foolish? Could someone else hurt you less? love you more? I love you, Nora. I adore you. But sometimes I want to sleep with other women. That's my story: You decide if you can accept it.

Jesus.

We are standing in the hall of our new apartment, admiring the twelve etched panes of glass in the front door as they flash in summer's first electrical storm. Robin takes my hand.

We are standing before the hall mirror, admiring its glints and scratches. Robin pushes me gently toward it.

Look at your beauty.

I raise up my eyebrows. Thunder cracks. I turn my profile from left to right, arguing for her benefit the preferability of the one over the other. She winks at me. I lean in and open my mouth, display in a mock censorious grin the perfect teeth I have inherited from Myra.

She slips her hand into her pocket and pulls out a small blue velvet box. Bright distance is lit by a lightning bolt.

No, I say, sucking air through my bared teeth.

Let me finish, she replies.

No, I say again.

When my mother died, my father gave me her ring. It does not suit me to wear it.

No, I say a third time.

You are my home now, sweet girl, she says, kissing my stolen mouth.

Robin announces she has fucked another woman. She tells me she won't condemn. Condemn who? She says she wants me to stay around and be Home but that sometimes from now on a shadow will fall on our bed.

No. She doesn't say that.

She looks at me in silence, then asks, Do you want to talk to me? She has a horror of these kinds of conversations.

What about? I say.

I want to throw hot coffee on her throat.

Autumn comes and sometimes she uses a particular turn of phrase that is new, totally innocent of the darkness leaping into me. Once she goes to a movie with a woman I have never met and I spend the evening with my hands between my thighs, rocking.

There is no Way that I am, there is no Way to live these hours. Love, as it leaves, leaves a memory of its weight. I am waiting, waiting, in useless circularity, for Robin to call my name even in the afterimage of my own refusal; while Robin, who comes from a world to which she is now returning, waits for me to follow.

We Are All Like This, Nora.

Can I defend that I am not?

Robin and I go to a party. We both drink a lot of free champagne and Robin flirts with every woman there. I sit by the fire, smoking, something I have begun to do again. Robin comes over from time to time to ask how I am doing.

Fine, baby, I'm fine, I say.

My friend Rae dances with Robin who tells her, Girlfriend is fine, and Rae scolds, You'll be lucky if you have a girlfriend after tonight. This really pisses Robin off. She says, That is just repressive thinking. That is lies. We Are All Like This.

I make a real effort to find out just how many are

looking to act on the sexy feelings that can come at the same time someone is waiting dinner on you. I watch how some women drop their hands between strange thighs and come up laughing. I watch a girl in black ripped stockings crawl up and down the beam a man sends her behind his wife's back, how another draws forward into the crevices of a woman's doubling words, and it is like it is on airplanes when too many passengers are inebriated and roaring above the cabin pitch even before the wing falls off mid-air and we are spinning out of control.

All that I have been taught to rely on, all of love's virtues, all the banners worn across the heart: We are dismantled, Robin and me. All the family portraits on the wall are beginning to slide like rain.

While I stand in the shadows preparing to leave the party, Robin talks to a woman who is leaning against the living room wall, smoking a cigarette, twisting her elegant neck away from Robin to blow perfect smoke rings over their heads. I can tell by the look of serenity spreading across Robin's handsome face that she is highly aroused.

Djuna is hovering above them, laughing like a banshee.

I walk home across the empty downtown streets and over the mountain, beneath the crushing night sky. I stand in front of the apartment on the chilled damp sidewalk, gazing up at our dimly lit front window. I wait until the need to piss overtakes me. Then I climb the stairs and push my key into its quiet lock.

≈

Jeff dies two hours after your arrival in Vancouver. You sit next to him through those hours, a large man whittled down by cancer. You hold his one hand and toy with his bloodstone ring, remembering his arm bent out the open window of the old Pontiac, your unasked questions the distance between you as you travel the full stretch of highway between Port Credit and Vancouver, photographer and subject. Why the night, Jeff? Why all this running away?

Jeff?

He seems to know you.

Do you have no shame?

What?

Is there nothing you have done?

What?

Tell me who you are.

I believe in everlasting life, he whispers. His last breath spins the room.

You want to ask Myra if, once alone with the dead Jeff in that hospital room, she had climbed onto him, or pulled the cotton gown back to gaze down on his shrunken body, his white flesh loose on raging bones. After Jeff dies, you want to stay with his body, travel with his silence into the great crematorium fire, assure yourself of his ashes. You continue to wait for some utterance from him, some quiet walk with him in Myra's garden, and you know you wait in vain. The part of Nora that will follow after Jeff, leaving her home veiled in the dark, collapses in an elegant swoon.

On Friday nights in the winters of my childhood, we go skating on the Credit River. I wear slacks under my leggings, a knitted sweater beneath my red ski jacket. Hat. Scarf. Mittens. The moist breath lodged in wool. Port Credit. Five-mile Friday night jagged skate inland and back, our faces pressed against the wind, to hot chocolate and bonfire sparks, background a starry Ontario night.

How insulated we were above the moving waters.

I hold Jeff's hand, moist mitten in black leather as we skate toward that inevitable signal that turns us back, a community of one hundred skaters destined between two points on a frozen line out of night.

But I've skated further and further away from that same community into a self that cannot open to the elixir of night air, the swish of blades, the unknowable. Nora has skated, alone and unrecognizable, to this burning orange place with its black stars, to a place Myra calls private.

Trickster work. To break this body down into world without end.

Djuna is holding one of my pictures in her hand. Did I ever tell you about my friend Emily Coleman? she asks. The last time I saw her, the first time in twenty years or more, she seemed erased. I dare say I seemed the same to her. I said, Would you have known me? She answered, No, except for the eyes. I don't think, had I passed her on the street, I would have known her at all. She did not seem mournful, but neither did she seem to have listed in her mind the passing of her life.

I am watching a young girl across the street plant seeds in her mother's garden. Her mother shows her how. The girl pats the wet soil with her dirty hands.

Was someone with you when you died, Djuna? I ask, turning from the window.

A nurse.

Were you frightened?

I'd once said I'd probably scream my lungs out and hang on like a cat on a curtain. But I didn't. I just walked into the photograph.

You walk to the edge of Mont Royal one night and peer down to the Plateau, to the streets where Robin roams. You know Robin is out there and you scan for her in the cool view. So many lights twinkle through the waves of shifting shadows on brilliant shining streets, it is hard to make out a particular light in any particular glass, framing your new lover's silhouette, the possibility of her hands circled round the bare hips of another woman, the two of them laughing, never thinking of you, like a sharp thorn catching you unexpectedly in the soft issue seeping away from your clutched throat.

Myra, I begin, why does a person hide all their love behind an opened newspaper, behind all the words they mean to say but never do?

Men are less secure about expressing emotions, Nora. Did you ever try loving the man behind?

I'm not just talking about Jeff.

Well?

Myra, now the widow, hunched, smaller, the sun almost liquid behind her, golden, its light slanting through the trees, a veil of dust on the rise. The black silhouettes of stumps and roots look like children waiting at her feet for a story. I can make out the calm line of a more quiet ocean.

There's a price for what you say you want, Nora.

What price?

Myra clutches her hands together in her lap, looking beyond me into the shadows.

Listen, I won't fight. Let's not fight. What's gotten into you? Your father's dead.

I sit down on a cold stone and look into my hands. Myra, how did you stay with Jeff all these years, I say.

Myra lifts her chest, shoulders down. There is no explanation for it.

A lifetime of little deaths. And the secrets? How have you explained those?

There may be some things you don't understand about my relationship with your father. Not everything is for public consumption, you know.

I'm not public.

Nora.

Tell me.

We were alive and together all these years. That must tell you something.

O, Mom, I say, wishing for all the world to stop myself but unable to do it. Alive? Alive? This family has a will to lock itself in tidy closets and sealed-off coffins.

How nice.

Was I ever a well-adjusted girl, swallowing my words, burying them in a smile, in an outfit with a nice pair of high heels? That afternoon, I swallow, I smile. I look away

89

toward the dark ocean through the shadowless trees.

C'mon, Myra, it's getting cold.

The next morning we sit in her kitchen eating oranges and brown toast and drinking percolated coffee, treating each other with shamefaced diffidence. Myra asks me to choose from among the objects in the house something of Jeff's to take with me. I walk among them — among black lacquered boxes and Flood family bird cages, among the Robert Louis Stevenson — searching for something. My fear runs below the task, and it is this: One day Myra will make her final exit, will no longer dig in her perfect garden, and on that day Grace and I will stand alone in a house of secrets and sliding silence.

In my hand I hold an orange glass with raised black dots, one I sent to Myra long ago. I had wanted her to find it as beautiful as I found it, but on my next trip to Kitsilano, I discover the glass put away in a kitchen cupboard. I console myself with the thought that Myra must see it every day, reaching for her coffee cup, and that the cupboard held its fragile beauty safe and, therefore, more truly. The consolation is brief and false. This day I notice it, admire it. Want it. The orange glass, hollering with the dangerous life within me.

I take the glass from Myra's cupboard, steal it away among my things, and tell Myra there is nothing of Jeff's I am prepared to take.

⁂

We walk through her garden and she points out her roses, calling each by its popular name. Maiden's Blush. Champlain. Alchymist. White Bath. Jens Munk. Jeff's insistent hollow voice is everywhere.

Help me, he cries.

Myra drives me to the airport. She tells me about her favourite rose, Heritage. Its petals are so delicate, Nora. Clear, almost. Pink. It blooms repeatedly.

Lucky you have your garden, I say.

After a few days home in Montreal I stand at the front window, lost, dry, sliding, and watch an injured cat die. I do nothing. I walk to the studio, try to set it for a photograph, but end up hurling ice cubes out the window into the night sky. I am desperate to read something familiar. I return home, scan the bulging shelves which hold, as well as my own, all the books Rae has given to me. Rae detests possessions. They weigh her down, she says.

C'mon, Nora, it's time to burn these fucking books. Your apartment is starting to smell like a bloody forest.

I remember sending Myra a novel Rae had given me, and when Myra finished it, she wrote to me: Nothing at all happened in that novel, not one thing happened.

My well-concealed garden, blooming repeatedly in its tidy little space. Where nothing happens. I exist in the skin and word and winter of Robin. Strange breed. Not Heritage, but yet not weed. What, then? It is hard to explain the social usefulness of staying with Robin, trailing arbutus in an unforgiving cultivated garden, Jeff pounding at the door, shouting, Blow out that goddamn candle, Nora, for chrissakes.

When you were ten you showed Jeff a poem you had written. He returned it to you with a red circle around a word misspelled: Separate. You, unlike Robin, have no Way that you are Like. You seem to want attachment to something staid, static, dead, safe, stopped. And then you want to leave for somewhere, out into the hostile world where the Nothing that you get is what you expect. But here, here, Robin's tongue now trailing the uncultivated garden, what are you planning to do, Nora, you with your infinite capacity for pain and your high-handed refusal to learn how to leave it?

There is no Way to do it, no Way that leaving's done.

You discover that Thelma loves intrigue and mystery and all things of the night. She infuriates you, and you find yourself trying to get inside her by imagining her improbable stories. If you speak at all, you babble, tell falsehoods, feel hot with shame in front of her but keep on, hating all that shaking humiliation. She sits quietly on Donny's faded pea-green velvet couch, smoking cigarettes, sipping red wine, one leg folded up beneath her, her arm resting on the back of the couch. Her eyes shift and squint, her magnificent eyebrows lift or furrow, but she does not interject, never interrupts. Never smiles a wide full smile. She smirks, refusing her own unsteady nerves.

Thelma leans out of frame, Donny explains.

She's jealous?

She's in love with you. Or, she's completely fucked. She's the inside of a mirror, the pith of lemon rind.

Donny, some situations don't call for rhyme. Okay?

And what about your photography? you ask one evening at Theodora's. Why not try to sell your work?

No. I don't want to live on it, I don't even want to show it, not like Donny, with his fucking scribbling.

You say nothing.

Donny says, You wait, Thelma. Nora will do something great one day, but not for the exact same reasons you take your dirty pictures, and certainly not for the reasons I scribble; to manage melancholy and insomnia.

You write to prove you're a man, Thelma says.

That night when you return home Jeff is waiting up for you in the living room.

Your mother and I have decided that this behaviour

93

of yours cannot continue, young lady. You think about nothing but yourself. It is obvious you do not think of us, or Grace, at all. When you live on your own you can —

I'll live on my own then.

On what? You haven't got a cent!

I'll get a job. In the evenings.

O, for chrissakes, Nora! You'll be the death of your mother.

Jefferson —

You keep your voice down.

You aren't shouting. Jeff is shouting. Soon Grace and Myra come downstairs to see what all the racket is about.

Jeff's upset because I told him I was moving out.

When? Myra says.

Are you pregnant? Grace asks.

I don't know, you say, looking down at your boots, too clean under the circumstances.

Don't be insolent, young lady. You're not too big to put over my knee, you know.

O, Da-a-a-d, Grace whines.

Myra peers at Jeff out of the corners of her eyes. Well, she says to you, you've made your bed!

Myra, listen —

No, you listen! There will be no coming back here begging for a meal, no crying about how expensive everything is. If you're out, you're out. I don't need you.

I don't need any of you. You could all up and leave me and I'd be all right. I figured that much out a long time ago. So off you go, Nora Flood, and let's see if you find living on your own any picnic.

Myra turns and pads back up the carpeted stairs in her mules.

By four in the morning you know: She is not coming home. This is not punishment for the suitcase. It has begun to snow, hard. The streets have disappeared.

So. You don't have to see Robin tonight, for which you are thankful. You are spared the shame of your own uncertainty, you can bed your own righteousness with a bottle of scotch. Alone.

Enter trouble.

Are words the high relief of the living within?

Is language steam released by a pressure gauge?

Are words property of the public thoroughfares only, or is there a little corner of uncommodified space in consciousness?

Is there a true, authentic self?

Can self be handled, palpable as a chicken breast?

Is identity meat or the heat beneath it?

Who goes blind the moment I open my mouth?

There has been a storm overnight, the streets are ploughed, the sky is blue. The weather report says the storm is not over yet, that a third act will follow before noon, the snow will fall down, heavy, like winter sheets; like the earth I am pounded, and shining. Robin has not come home.

Please come flying, this fragment will not leave me and my wretched hangover alone. But what is the point of my obsession if not to turn my manners to stone?

After I set up the tripod in the bathroom, after I load a new roll of film into the Nikon, after I wash the dishes and empty the ashtrays, put away the bottle of Johnny Walker and make the bed, I call Rae. I congratulate myself on taking this ordinary step while Rae's phone rings: Everyday women whose hearts are breaking call their women friends and talk about their problems. Everyday women who are thinking of leaving their partners call their friends to discuss options. Everyday women know that if their lovers do not come flying home before morning, they should not immediately blame the weather.

Good morning, says the voice on the other end of the line, and it is Robin.

Jesus Christ. You fucking bitch. *Rae*.

A small brown bird takes flight from my chest, and I

hang up.

I fumble in the hall closet for a fresh towel. I stand in front of the hall mirror, catching a brief scent of Robin in the disturbed dust motes that rise above the ruckus I am making with my feet. My naked flesh begins to slide.

Djuna Barnes lived forty years on Patchin Place, with the intense burning loneliness of superiority.

Your home is on fire, tell me, will you flee?

FOUR

This is me, lying half dead on the divan, listening for something, listening to the upstairs neighbour's brilliant piano improvisation rising above the tires spinning in the icy streets below, this is me moving the tiny bones in my wrist to the beat on the piano, thinking of death. This is me reading me: You want to be good, to be generous. This is me reading Robin in this other, darker hour: Hate.

If you knew for certain that no one watched, no one applauded your goodness and generosity, your spirited improvisation, would you still find it so intoxicating? Or would you begin to look for a way to move out into the world?

After you are gone, no one will remember you or want you.

❧

You move into Thelma's apartment on Burrard. Myra and Jeff give you a twin bed and dresser, and the reading lamp you had hauled in and out of your closet after Jefferson finally forbade the candle and its dangerous flame. On moving day, Jeff lowers his paper from time to time to watch Grace and you carry your things out to the car, but he does not get out of his armchair. Myra pretends to weed her perfect garden.

See you, Myra! you call to the crumpled figure in the rose bed.

Myra turns. Don't think you can plop your dirty laundry on my floor any time you feel like it, she yells. If you're going, you're going.

White bars of Ivory soap hang in your memory.

You unpack your books and journals while Thelma sits on the edge of your bed, drinking black coffee.

Dostoevsky? Did you like this?

Loved it. Have you read *The Idiot*?

No. I don't read books written by men.

What do you mean?

Men. You know, people with pricks. I don't read their shit.

But you listen to Donny's stuff all the time.

I don't listen. Not really.

You can't understand this. Maybe it explains her lurid career as men's night photographer, always risking, never caring what of theirs would land inside a picture and what would land out. Tracking the silence of men, her pictures full of shadowy night figures in flagrant stature, men embracing under bridges and in parks, homeless men lolling, men cruising the prostitutes on Davie. You suspect she sees more in the moonlight than she lets on. You ask her if you can go out shooting with her one night, partly to change the subject.

If you like, is all she says.

❀

Thelma never takes me with her. But sometimes she meets me for coffee in the all-night doughnut shop where I work. Thelma is coiled; I can smell her tension, a damp salty heat mixing with the stench of grease that clings to my dirty uniform, its burgundy collar stiff with dried sweat. Where are you going now, Thel? I ask, knowing she will lie.

Over to English Bay, she answers, fidgeting with her lens cover, folding and unfolding the camera strap.

What time will you be home?

You'll see me when you see me.

The hardest thing is to come home to an empty apartment after a day of school and a night of orders and sit at my desk in the yellow light, wanting to do something and feeling so tired. More often than not, I lay my head down and weep myself to sleep, waking with a start when Thelma's key turns in the lock. Hello kid, she says, all soft and careful. Sometimes after shooting Thelma turns sweet. You want to have a beer with me? she says. And I agree to one, perched on the side of her bed telling her about my day, believing that when she opens her covers and invites me in, I will be home.

Sometimes Thelma brings men back to our apartment late at night. My head shoots up from my desk, my ears stiff as a cat's. The stink coming off Thelma makes me turn out my light and retreat to my narrow twin bed, gathering the dark silence into my chest as I lie absolutely still, hoping she will think me asleep. How many nights do I listen to the cruelties beyond the next wall? How many pieces of glass scatter across hardwood floors as wasted hands relax their hold?

I watch Thelma in a room; a party. She gathers all light to her, courts the living light in every man and in every woman, she speaks neither one true nor one unkind word; her body is motion, her electrical field is flame. I am too close to her; because of her, something shape-shifts within me. I hug the walls of the room, trying to lay claim to what it is about Thelma that has me in its teeth.

Does she have my light, or do I have hers?

After graduation from high school, I work full time at a coffee shop. Grace meets and marries an egg farmer and moves to Salt Spring Island to raise chickens and babies.

You're a libber and a vegetarian, Nora, she cautions when I raise my eyebrows. What do you know?

I remember a summer blue sky arching above Jeannette's steamer carpet, the rich earth crawling with life beneath me as I lie on my back watching black spots of circling birds mix with the floaters on my cornea in one dizzying dance. How Jeannette pauses from her reading to watch my eyes crossing and sweeping and dipping, my mouth opened, before she quietly draws up into her straw a suck of milk from her thermos, dangles the straw over my outstretched body, then blasts the milk in gorgeous shower upon my warm seven-year-old legs.

Oops! she says, as I scramble up onto my knees and roll on top of her.

Jeannette! I cry.

She flashes her big teeth at the sun.

I watch Thelma rewind her film, her long strong fingers curled around the body of her camera. Where does she go each night? I try to live up to my own expectations of what the best of me might look like, loving Thelma.

Take my picture.

One night during a party at Donny's, after drinking too much scotch and Thelma threatening to burn all Donny's poetry if he writes one more word, she suddenly comes over to me and puts her tongue down my throat. I turn my face away and push her, hard, on the shoulders; she stumbles and falls backwards onto the floor.

What do you think you're doing?

Doing you a favour, she says, wiping the back of her hand across her mouth.

O, yeah? What's that?

You can't be a virgin all your fucking life, Nora.

My god, you're good, Donny says, offering his hand to Thelma, his face in hers as he helps her to her feet.

Fuck off, you little queen.

Temper, temper, teacher, teacher. C'mon, Nora darling. Let Thelma stew in her own hot juices.

In the bathroom, I break down in Donny's arms.

Why is she so mean? She says I'm her best friend, can you believe it. Her best friend! She treats me like a child. I'm twenty years old.

And a virgin.

So fucking what!

No fucking, you mean, which seems to annoy Miss Thelma to this point of insurrection. Tell me, Nora, have you figured out whether you like boys or girls?

I'm not sure I like either.

For once Donny holds his tongue.

But why is everyone in such a big hurry to get me to bed? It was you who told me to give up believing in time.

Yes, Donny says, resting his chin on my shoulder, his arms still around me. But maybe it's impossible to give up time without giving up the body, too.

O, Donny, I cry, tears filling my mouth.

What words, honey? he asks.

Move, I say.

I pace the floor between sink and window, a tiny circuit dance around Donny, my heart beating so fast that I try to move to its beat and even beyond it. I move back into Donny's solid embrace, a terrible loneliness overtaking me. O, Donny, I cry, over and over. O, Donny. And then his mouth is on my mouth and my mouth is hungry. I see pure space before me, in its vast endless field the unassuming future. Then our clothes are falling down and Donny is deep inside me, and I am giving up my body, my gaze focused on nothing, seeing beyond him. When we pull back from one another, he looks at me, serenely, unencumbered.

Nora?

Donny?

We see each other, through and through. And I am terrified.

I walk home alone that night, my legs thick below me, my torso swooping then skimming the tops of the grasses that edge the pavement, like a swallow protecting its nest. I vow not to tell Thelma what has happened. The word Move is discernible in the bed of stars overhead.

I call Donny the next afternoon. Before I can manage a second word, he says, Are you all right, honey?

Is that sex? I ask.

That is love, he answers, after a while.

In less than two months I board a train for Toronto, my worldly goods packed into six wooden fish crates, a pink pyjama bag shaped like a pig tucked under my arm. Leaving, and breaking.

Will you write me, Donny?

I'm a wretched correspondent, darling.

Postcards?

I'll try. I won't promise, but I'll try. But you write me. Describe those gorgeous boys on Yonge Street in severe detail. And whatever happens, darling, keep believing in words. They are, after me, your best friend.

Do you love me, Donny?

Sweet boy, you are the joy of my life.

He thrusts a package into my hands then pushes me up the train car's wrought iron steps. When I turn around in the space between the cars, he is already flying down

the platform away from me, his black cape twisting up
into the air like one misshapen wing.

I find a seat in the coach and throw myself into it.
As the train pulls away and my tears subside, I open the
package: Arthur Rimbaud's *Illuminations*. And inside
the front cover, in Donny's sprawling hand:

*When we are very strong, — who draws back? very gay,
— who cares for ridicule? When we are very bad, — what
would they do with us? Deck yourself, dance, laugh. I
could never throw Love out of the window.*

She who thinks deeply, who moves in public space, who
resists the fairy tale, achieving a muscularity in her
feminine willfulness: I am not this Nora Flood.

Approach Nora Flood. Approach the tears that begin
to run down her face.

Now I take up again the tracking of light and
shadow, less distracted by questions of sufficiency. Stars
augment. Now I move into the night streets with my
eye pressed capriciously to my camera, now I climb the
streets looking for the thing that is there, which exists,
which can be handled and left to itself. Now I say: I am
observer, I am recorder. Nothing will be changed. Now
I say the other's name out loud — Robin — she who is

two — and Robin waits for me while another Nora tracks the position of the moon, to whose face like a frog she clings.

You move in temporarily with Alice, into the room where Grace and you slept during weekend visits, now a small sewing room, Alice's endless church projects — aprons and quilt pieces — strewn across the old Singer table like a soft storm of white cotton. There remains the small, much-loved divan that pulls apart into two narrow beds, and the old oak desk with its tiny secret compartments, and if you turn over one corner of the carpet you can still read the place in the hardwood floor where Grace and you scratched a line from *Leaves of Grass*. You think Grace would find the memory impenetrable now.

Alice's room is at the far end of the narrow dim hall. You like to sit on the end of her single bed and look at the old black and white family photographs on the walls; the one of Alice frowning and John turning away, their arms around each other, standing on a dock above misty Oban Lake; Myra in nurse's cap at her graduation, her mouth open, flashing her perfect teeth; Grace, Jeannette, the two cousins and you, arms akimbo, chests inflated, posing in your bathing suits and plastic bathing caps in a Haliburton lake, the only picture of Jeannette still hanging on any wall. You rifle through Alice's dresser drawers, anxious that you should do something about the stained underwear there. You stretch out on her eiderdown with your hands behind your head and study the plaster gargoyle circling the overhead light. Sometimes you sit at her vanity table and brush your short hair with her silver soft-bristled brush, gazing beyond your reflection to the heavy black rotary dial telephone on Alice's bedside, the phone you use to speak to Myra when you call long-distance.

Have you been looking for work? Have you found an apartment?

You take a job at a coffee shop on Yonge Street, and it isn't long before you learn the whereabouts of a gay bar around the corner, discreetly stashed in a lane behind a Bloor Street warehouse. The coffee shop is analgesic to gay hangovers. Your second day on the job, two male customers joke about diesel dykes while you stand above them, pouring coffee into porcelain mugs. They lean together whispering vulgarities, smoking their cigarettes with campy panache, then stop their conversation to ask you if you know who has the ruby slippers.

Donny, you say, snapping up their menus.

Ouch, little sister, they bellow, did we touch a nerve?

Do you know the Japanese expression? you ask.

They shake their heads.

One boy alone is one boy, two boys together is half a boy, and three boys together is no boy at all.

They exchange glances.

The girl's funny, one says.

His friend looks at you. Yeah, but is she funny *that way*?

You begin to drink a little scotch at the gay bar after work to dampen your longing for Donny and Thelma, and to make the quiet evenings with Alice a little more bearable, when together you watch old movies on her black and white TV. *Night of the Iguana*. *All About Eve*. You run along the actresses' words, out into a future bordered on the one side by tedium, on the other by repulsiveness. Alice tries to entwine your two hearts.

Nora. Do you miss Jeannette? She might have helped you. An older sister can help sometimes.

You find a bachelor apartment in the west end and Alice gives you the divan and a lamp to take into the tedium. In the evenings, wasted from too much scotch, weak from too little food, you lie on the divan asking, What words? but the moving water is mute.

At twenty, you can make no use of Nothing.

Perhaps survival itself resembles greatness. To have the fortitude for nothing, the vast emptiness. And perhaps you achieve your greatness — or rather, not you but someone else, just as Djuna Barnes had said.

❧

You watch the light and shadow, how they travel across the worn hardwood floor of the home you are not making, far from expectation or design. You watch how the morning light turns from green to scarlet in its orbit across the dormer windows, like a northern lake there, dawn passing wildly to day. You think about light and then you imagine a camera. A good camera. One that could carry you through the years, one that could keep the record.

An image of Thelma rises up in you like a wire.

You buy a cheap Pentax, a roll of Tri-Pan X, a used copy of John Berger's *Ways of Seeing* — and to remind yourself of who and what you are, a bottle of Johnny Walker Red — and begin the transference of light to love. Your first photos follow the tracks of late-night rhomboids, golden suitcases jerking across the floor at the base of the dormer window, moving on. The alchemic process turns these travelling quadrangles of gold into pearly traps, doors to the universe. The photos begin to show both what you see and what you might have seen had you been less blind.

The ways of seeing are reciprocal. A photo reciprocates.

How swiftly the colours of autumn turn to grey rain and grey days. Your imagination takes flight. What is it about shadow that seems to refuse light?

Sometimes the viewfinder presses against your eye in such a way as to make you think that you will never find anyone, that there will never be anyone to take an interest in you. Then you take the picture.

Sometimes you watch the train of ghostly light move across the dormer windows like an angelic bellowing. Strange it is. A hypnotic late-night light show scored by passing cars below.

Mesmerized, unseemly to yourself, you watch the light show. Entertained and despondent. Not a twitch of initiative in the heart-shocked flesh holding you together.

And this goes on.

Many nights you sprawl, dead on the divan, drunk, desiccated, grotesque. Helpless in a crib of passing light, an orphan in her torture chamber. Alone, calcifying. Assaulted.

You begin to forego your trips to the bar, come home after work to pour yourself a plentiful Johnny Walker and carry on with the document of your despair which is fast becoming a series of contact strips pinned to the wall next to the divan.

You read Michael Ondaatje, and *Zen and the Art of Motorcycle Maintenance*. You don't pretend to understand the half of it, and ignore good advice to put a book down if it is not immediately compelling. You wonder if you are trying anything in your own way.

Maybe our whole lives we spend garnering love.

You are falling in love with light. The way it jumps through your window at 6:38 am. The dazzling sunlight, the weight of its rays pouring down on your crossed eyes as you lie on your side waiting for it to arrive as maybe one waits for a lover, through all the mornings of milky clouds and thunderstorms and mist and tears. And you wonder if anyone really ever can be up to the task of love, and if so then how come you don't know about it?

You take some books out of the library and read up on Thelma's specialty, night light. There is quite a bit of it, it turns out. Enough to forego a flash, as Thelma knew.

All desire is insatiable and ultimately narcissistic. I moved into Patchin Place to live out the last forty-two years of my life alone. It was a little bachelor apartment: I had a tiny kitchenette behind a curtain, and an open fireplace. E.E. Cummings and his wife lived downstairs at number four.

Djuna is looking over contact sheets hanging above the divan. Her lip curls slightly, a sneer which she tries to hide behind a cough.

Heard from your old pansy recently? she asks.

You move into a tiny apartment near High Park. You beg your camera and its lens to reveal to you their secrets, to reveal the accumulations of twenty years, the objects you looked on, then became.

113

And then they do.

You walk the beach at Sunnyside after dark, a student of sound and audible season. Djuna visits you there, appearing, disappearing, reappearing, with heavy shoes and a quick wit, wrinkled, in an old coat of gaberdine, inventing you over and over, but as you walk home again past the darkened shop windows on Roncesvalles, you refuse all reflection.

Trains go by, blowing; letters from Donny come and go. Visions wake you in the night, troubling, full of half-light and half-meanings. Myra knocks at your pride, but you will not answer. Nobody knows how you argue with yourself.

Myra calls and you are drunk.

Your father is coming to Toronto on Thursday. He's staying at Sutton Place. Get him to take you out for a good meal. You need to eat.

I'm eating.

Do you need any money?

We've gone over this before. No handouts.

Nora. Please. Are you looking after yourself?

Look, when Jeff gets here I'll make him buy me plates and plates of filet mignon.

✧

You save up your pathetic tips and buy a brand new Nikon at a place on Queen Street East where the staff treat you like the greenhorn you are. The Pentax has served its purpose. The guy who talks you into the Nikon is frumpy and mean-spirited. As you leave the shop — as if carried by angels across a great divide — you trip on the curb but catch the camera as it wings out in a magnificent arc before you fall with it onto the sidewalk.

There's glass in that thing, the guy shouts from the doorway of the shop where he stands smoking, watching you. Be careful, for chrissakes.

You know you are copying Thelma, and your lack of ingenuity irks you, but you take to the night streets with the new camera and snap furtive pictures of gay men. The boys at the café drop hints about where the action might be — Rosedale Valley Road, St James Cemetery, the woods at the foot of Riverdale Farm — and you are ashamed because you do not understand the roots of your growing compulsion, do not understand the angry thrusts of your pelvis against a pillow you tuck between your thighs each night on your return, calling out in your wolfish agony before falling into a troubled sleep: Donny.

Love, love, love. You chant under your breath throughout all the terrible days serving coffee on Yonge

Street. Light, light, light, you whisper in the streets under lamplight, waiting for the boys.

And then one soft summer night below the city in the deep green ravine — a night without wind, the full moon at rest overhead — you see him through your one-eyed gaze — Jefferson — in the arms of another man. His hand is cupped tenderly behind the other's head, his tongue quietly explores the other's mouth. He is naked, except for a cock ring. Gold glints converge into your elaborate eye that now pulls quickly away from the camera, like a visor torn from what was once your smooth face. With your head turning toward the silver-lined woods that crown the ravine, your camera still pointing toward him, you take his picture.

The day is fine. A fleet of sailboats dots the horizon. There is a slight breeze which breaks like cool water on the skin. Djuna is dabbling her feet in the lake. Her shoes and stockings are draped over her black purse behind her on the small pier.

What did you drink? I ask her.

Gin, mostly. Too much whiskey. And I smoked Chesterfields. Lots of them. I always carried matches in my pockets.

I don't want to end up like you, Djuna.

What? You mean dead?

Haha. But, well, yes. Dead. Dead and drunk in a little drunk woman's space, broken by delirium, stumbling to the back rooms of local lesbian shopkeepers who fix you up with another gin in order to send you home again.

Jesus. Is that what it looks like from here? I suppose it was perverse.

I'm afraid I *could* end up like you. Do you know how I'll end up?

No, I don't.

You don't?

Who can know? You're so hell-bent on liberation. But you could end up like Virginia Woolf.

If I could take just one photograph that even began to approach the beauty of Woolf's *Between the Acts*, I'd die happy, I say.

Djuna rises from the pier and stretches, dissolves then reappears in the top branches of a gingko tree behind us, next to the beach pavilion, rolling one silk stocking up over one thick calf.

What about that photo you took of Jefferson? she calls to me.

What about it? I yell, furious, and Djuna disappears for a long time.

Have you figured out yet whether you like boys or girls, Nora?

Donny asks this question at the opening of our long-distance conversation.

I don't want to bring anyone up to my apartment.

Why? What's wrong with it?

It smells like developer. From the photos.

Honey, it's your perfect opportunity: Tell them it's chemistry, he says.

Haha. Shut up. I miss you, Donny.

Have you met anyone? he wants to know.

How can I meet anyone if I don't know who I like? Where should I go to meet them?

Yes, he sighs. All this rejection, rejection. I blames the militant dykes, I does. We need mixed bars, to learn inclusion and respect, not all these fucking lezzie-only bars.

Donny, I say. What do you have on right now?

What?

What are you wearing?

My purple tie-dyed caftan.

How long is your hair?

Long. It's really beautiful now, Nora.

You're so square, I say.

What? What do you mean?

If I start to date boys, Donny, they probably won't be gay boys.

Not gay? He seems to choke on this. That's absurd.

Well, I say. We'll see. And while we're at it, I should clear up another thing: Not everyone reads poetry, you know, or even cares about it. For your information, there are people who don't even know who Rimbaud was.

Land sakes, child. What are they teaching you in Toronto? You best get home right away.

In the first morning the world is clean and white. After fresh croissants and bowl after bowl of café au lait, you roll together among the crumbs in your bed. You massage her pale and narrow feet.

You are promised Nothing: Nothing is given to us, Nora, she says.

She reads you a poem from a book that she's pulled off your shelf, she lies back against three pillows and reads you a love poem while a mouse darts back and forth along the baseboards with something in its mouth. Snow falls like white feathers, the world is shining all its colours like ice beyond your window. You get a little dreamy thinking about the poem and about Robin reading poetry, it seems inconceivable to you that someone could read a poem about love and yearning out loud on the first day of this new year, to you, a girl

119

with mice running amok in her one-and-a-half.

You do not think of Donny.

Dear Nora,

I am very glad to know that someone in Montreal has taken an interest in you, but I must say I am completely baffled by you, saying you are grateful. Grateful? When you are down to your last dime and a stranger hands you a couple of dollars or takes you out for a drink and a meal, be grateful. In matters of love, however, don't make the mistake most of us make. She is not doing you a kindness, sweet boy! If this Robin does not give you the moon, the stars and all the planets, I will personally travel to wherever she is and hurl her so far into the cosmos, they'll have to pump light to her.

It can stand repeating: She better be good to you. Leave her the second she errs.

All my love,
Donny

You are already undressed and stand discreetly by the window, naked. She is a little late. It is snowing, a heavy accumulation weighing down the leafless tree outside your window. A small brown bird lends its wing to the heaving branches, rises up then addresses itself to the warmth of its own feathers. Hunkers down.

You never knew it could thunder in winter.

She arrives at the foot of the iron steps, in her gloved hand she carries champagne in a brown paper bag. She fumbles in her trousers for the key you have given her. She is a picture.

You move away from the window to the front door and tabulate by the dim ring and strain of the stairs the exact progress of her arrival. At the entrance, she kicks her boots one at a time against the building and the thumping of the brick breaks into your chest. She removes her hat, runs her fingers through her hair, turns the key in the lock. Opens the door.

Nora, she says, dazzled.

I've given the servants the day off, you say.

She laughs. Let it snow, let it snow, let it snow.

Her large cold hand presses on your ready warm thigh, all pictures in your head collapse, a short hot needle pulls like stitches through your arms, cunt.

This is not silence, you think, your eyes closed. This is not closet.

Imagine blue, she says, her fingers deep within you,

your call breaking out of you, come-soaked, enthralled by its own voice, every shining object in your apartment reflecting the orange flame of two everlasting lives down on all fours.

Shame spreads your flesh like a knife.

Once I have developed the film to be sure it is Jefferson I saw in the Rosedale ravine, I write a very angry letter addressed to him, and spend an entire workday thinking about mailing it to him. How could you do this to Myra? At different times throughout the day, an effete faggot comes into the coffee shop and asks to speak to the owner. I usher each one of them into the back room, and close the door.

It is not unusual for coffee shop strangers to come and go all day, but that day my imagination goes a little wild. I know drug deals are being conducted behind the closed door, but instead I picture the boss and the stranger in the back office, naked, violent and bright. One of them always turns into Donny; one of them always turns into Jefferson.

That night I put the letter and the photograph of Jefferson into a small wooden incense box, take a small trowel from my tool box, and walk down to King Street and over the bridge that spans the Gardiner Expressway, to Sunnyside beach. Jeannette is waiting in the pavilion, reading Emily Dickinson at one of the marble tables. There is no one else in sight.

She watches as I dig beneath one of the gingko trees, my hand with the trowel disappearing into a small, deep hole until I reach water. I sit back on my haunches and meet her gaze, the box held tightly in my aching hand.

You will continue to find that it is almost impossible to bury things, Nora, she says.

I am sitting in the warm silent kitchen. The refrigerator hums, upstairs our neighbour is speaking excitedly to her lover. It reminds me of arguing, but no, in French it is only conversation, which I confuse with my own laboured arguments. Robin is out.

I sit here full-weighted with the way of all blessings heavy in my groin. I imagine Robin sucking on this heavy swelling, pulling me down through painful kitchen silence. Now the neighbour has stopped calling, now the refrigerator is quiet, now the only sound is the turn of a clothesline pulley down the lane.

I sit here wary of my heart's silence. It alerts me, not to her bait, not to the terrible possibility of her hook, but only to its own loss of hope. I prepare for her monologue;

legs shift, fabric faintly rustles; my eyes skim the room; and then her imagined voice, it is Robin's voice in the stillness and in her voice is my terrible knowledge that she has forgotten me.

It is Thanksgiving, *Action de grâce*. I make turkey. The succulent meat falls ready from its bones. I eat vegetarian paté and drink robust wine, I walk to the mountain and see two raccoons tame as anything begging for bread. I throw a stone into the darkness and listen for but do not hear the sound of stone landing on ground.

I am too sure of the distance to think I can change a thing, even if I lived in Robin's heart as she says I do. My belly drags me to the floor. I refuse to imagine how she will look, leaving, though a door closes over and over.

It is Robin's birthday today. I sit here with my unbearable mind and the hum of the city. I think of moments: Her strangeness whirling like dry leaves in a windswept ditch; my longing for a thing irrepressible and irreparable; our saying love out loud.

Does she feel my thoughts like a cool hand run along her naked side?

I sink down on our stories and I grow more cold in their telling.

I look closely at the photos I have taken of her throughout the years.

I am miles away from the side of her heart. For three years I have built a bridge between us that falls short of connection. I send out a plea to her, pegged to the clothesline on the pulley that swings widely, hauntingly, like the stretching pendulum tick of an old clock on an old mantelpiece in an almost-empty house in the middle of a silent night, calling to her heart, her groin, her dark centre: Just give me time to reach you.

I have nothing more. Not words, not heart, not imagination.

O, taste and see, says the hum of the night, the voice pouring down my thighs, pouring down these walls, pouring in the wings. The Greek chorus sings its chant of renewal while someone starves, blind to the long lace-covered table of turkey and stuffing, kiwi and pumpkin pie, whipped cream, persimmon, red wine, chestnuts and wild rice, candlelight, daisies, and a woman who stalks the crumbs.

How far does your compassion for Jefferson extend? Can you forgive the universe for what it has allowed him to do? Can you?

Can you look out at this mysterious night sky, look out at the Milky Way and the full moon and Orion's belt hanging loose before night's black scrim, the Nothing behind it hollering obscenities, look out over this winter pond with its icy rim crackling at midnight, with Djuna and Jeannette both watching you from the edge of the wood, there, both of them shining in the night, each one the silver outline of a white poplar in shadow in the moonlight, can you remember at one and the same time all the joy and all the pain hurled out at random and without compassion by the Nothing behind the curtain, to every single one of us, poor Jeannette, poor Djuna, can you embrace the unbearable truths of a cruel and beautiful universe?

Can you?

Too bright. Too bright!

Take this picture, take it now, take it here, in this nightwood.

Take it, Nora!

Was Donny the fool you were assigned through whom you were to learn the patterns of your life? Why have you forgotten him? How have you lived without him? You are in Montreal almost four years, have not spoken to Donny once in two years, and then one night on the Main, drunk on red wine, you with your camera slung around your neck stumble over an inebriated faggot in black cape bent down to tie his lace, the two of you tumble in the street, and then you sit up, see the static twitching in his long hair, lifting it up, and you begin to laugh.

Whasso funny? he asks.

Your hair. It's very fly-away. You remind me of someone, you say.

I look like any man, he says, pouting.

No. No, you do not. Come, let me buy you a drink.

You take him to La Cabane where the noise makes it almost impossible to talk. You shout questions at this man, trying to turn the sour night into a silk purse.

Do you believe in God?

I don't see why I should, he answers.

Have you ever loved a woman?

You hope he might say he's loved his mother for an hour here and there.

This man knows Donny out in Vancouver. He tells you that Donny published a first book of poetry the year before and that it sank without a trace. He tells you that Donny has become a recluse.

Once the next morning's hangover is deprived of its thorns, you call him.

Nora, he says. How I've missed you.

He tells you that he refuses most visitors now. He tells you about his companion, how this other man carries him from room to room while Donny trails his lightening blood. He tells you about the state of his liver and describes the purple lesions and tumours on his hands and face.

You fly out the next day.

❦

O, cry. Put your sweet face down among folds of white blanket, smell memory, the morphine lifting with each patterned breath now coming sure and hard and shallow, he can't stop it. O, cry. Put your hands on the metal side rail of the hospital bed and watch him dangle his open mouth, oxygen tube in nostrils faintly moist. O, cry memory, memory the plastic straw in his hungry mouth. O, cry, his hand on his heart as we lean out the open window of his False Creek loft.

Sing, my sweet boy. Sing!

Yellow morphine and urine.

Memory.

In hospital gown, shrunken, ancient silences. A struggle with light blue cotton, wet yellowish stink. Fresh cotton, his features realign into the face you want, there there. I love you. I love you, too. So much voice breaking, words crushed under waves, the years left unsaid.

Memory of light, that red morning distorting through the windows' frosted glass, a million mornings if you roll your head like a kaleidoscope, a million geometric sunrises.

Would you like a coffee? did we could we drink? would it go down? We change seats all day. Did someone knit a sweater? Hours pass, a plastic oxygen tube in his nose foggy then clear, foggy then clear.

Memory. Regular short breathing and then conges-
tion, abrupt, wet fluid in the air, a fish gagging. O, cry.
Tears racing, O, cry for the doctor who comes running
with a machine to suck out the fish, all of us gulping the
air. He moves his hand for the last time, pushes away the
sucking straw. Leave him alone! we scream, he is so
vulnerable one last time.

We wait.

O, cry, the gagging begins again, he isn't getting
breath, is he? is he? no O God he is lifting a soundless
chest a silent throat a wilderness of voice, is he? is he? O,
is he?

O, cry, the room is still we are none of us breathing,
someone help, O, beautiful Donny.

My beautiful Donny.

Let him go! he says, his friend, begging you. Let
him go. A thump from how your heart stops, letting
him go. Silent fool on a pillow not breathing lifting
settling leaving leaving, you are the lift and he is leaving
your chest thumping and his friend calling, Let him go,
let him go!

You.

Leaving.

O, cry. O, cry. This body consumed by words, these
eyes emptying, a new smell rising as all colour drains
away. He taught you to endure time and words, and you
are failing him.

Memory of the light of that red morning, the room now flooded with red. You stand at a window waiting, your stomach expanding as your chest rears up, the horse inside. You turn, Donny's friend is coming into the room and O so gently closing the door behind him.

You gallop, you walk slowly to him, wet and sweating, you put your arm around him and when you tell him the story you tell it slant.

In the morning Myra walks me around her garden. The things I didn't say to Donny are lodged in the spaces between my rib cage. Myra and I stand together admiring her roses. She draws my attention to a new addition, a wonderful Papa Meilland, Jeff's favourite. She puts her arm around my waist.

You are too thin, Nora, she says, not looking at me. Are you taking care of yourself?

I would like to tell her then all the things of my life.

When I return from Vancouver, Robin and I take a trip to Tadoussac, at the Saguenay, to see the blue whales spawning in the swirl where fresh water meets salt. At twenty-six, I cannot yet make use of what lies between us: I make the decision to stay on alone in a motel room and Robin goes back home. I stand out in the vast creaking silence the first night, watching how the stars are really pinpricks in black paper with a light behind, wanting to fly up praising those beautiful twinkling holes and suddenly I am tasting blood in my mouth.

Robin calls me from Montreal and tells me she has slept with another woman and is now thinking that what she really wants is to be loved by others as well as I love her so that if I die or leave she can still call Love and it will come. She Is Like This. She calls me from a phone booth, calls because she is thinking of me right there and then. How can I tell her I am fighting with something about myself I never even knew I had failed?

I tell her I am disappearing because I cannot eat and can barely sleep. I have had a running sex documentary going on in my head since the day she left. And then I scream at her all of a sudden that these women she lies down with are thieves, squatters and looters, stealing the only passion they have ever known, mine for Robin.

She knows these words, and tells me to put the book down.

Invent your own words, Nora, she says.

FIVE

Imagine *blue*, she says. A primitive blue, first colour. I imagine this blue rising from collarbone to skull top, an opened mind enthralled with voice as I cry in the shower and later on the slope of Mont Royal. I carry my camera. Nobody may hear me yet: This story is my bewildering secret.

My god, Myra, the pressing in my veins when I stand so new above this city, memory like a violent injection of homeblood. It is astonishing, this return of desire. Somewhere in the trajectory of my feverish memory, Mother, there is ground, there is a living earth, and if I am chosen, then this ground is where I will find love.

You walk the Sunnyside beach on summer nights when the air in your one-room apartment turns to dust. A dare to yourself. It is dangerous, and the dread you feel the first time turns into howling fear as your walking continues. Grace taunts you.

You won't keep it up. Flash in the pan. Once a coward, always a coward. Remember when I tied your hands to the railway track?

Shut up. I never told Myra about it. I could have.

Still trying to hold me on your knee, Nora?

You turn, and in a voice you try to keep steady say, Once I wanted you to die, I looked at you asleep in your little bed next to mine and I prayed that you would die so that my humiliation would end.

You walk the beach thinking about how love might turn your heart toward something further than tomorrow, the thought drawn into thin lines by your furtive scanning left and right. A black dog sniffs at your heels. Jeannette walks with you, or rather swoops along the water's edge, silently, watching. Djuna stands by a gingko tree, an ancient figure, gnarled, in old coat and shadow.

Grace is right. You do not believe you can keep this up. You contemplate the lake. You put two heavy stones into the pockets of your skirt, then stand on the shore in the lake's soft glaze beneath two thousand stars, composing the note. Then three geese pass directly across the face of the moon. You set the stones down and return home.

On Alice's eighty-ninth birthday you take the subway and bus to the edge of the city to see her. She lives in a nursing home now. After arranging cornflowers in the one vase she has — beige, dull, who brought her this ugliness? — you lie together on her bed, leaning against her three needlepoint pillows, all swirls of green and turquoise blue. You put your young arm around her, feel her damp neck against your flesh. The juxtaposition of her few belongings — warm wool, dark wood, her red crushed velvet chair the only piece brought from her home, even the bright aquamarine dress she wears — and the sterility of the metal walkers and wheelchairs and side rails, she takes these much better than you. You cling to a nostalgia that has no place here. Useless.

She repeats the story about her friend Earla Burke telling her where babies come from, and embarrasses herself. Shakes her head. You are bored and she knows it. She starts to tell stories about the nurses and the cleaning staff. They are poisoning her.

She says suddenly, I have to go to the ladies', in the middle of a sentence. Big uncertain flourish, scurry, shut the door after setting her gently on the toilet seat, her thighs cool in your hands. You didn't get your gifts from me, she shouts behind the door. Maybe from your grandfather.

And what you should have said then — but what could you say while blindsided by doubt? What gifts do you possess? You are wailing. The family portraits are grim on her wall.

What words?

Is this grief? To see every act instantly in introspection?

How can you keep your eyes trained on the world?

What can we call home, Father, in this car now moving over rises in the land, its tires swift against the pavement? A photograph catches the circles of its spinning wheels which blur into ellipses, the photographic moment irreconciled to the black and white cows at the gate, there, munching their cud; or to Djuna, drifting in surreal middle space, who just now points to a woman in a field with her child; or to that raven, now sweeping down from its perch high above us to cross in shadow the mother and child's little scene as the landscape turns a green-lit forty-five degrees and we are falling over the crest of this green hill.

You call leaving, *home*.

Who is the man in the photograph, Jefferson? I want to shout.

We each must be allowed our secrets, Nora.

Tell me. *Tell me.*

The raven mounting the sky is a consolation, the terrain we are passing through marked by glinting liquid in its fields which correspond in angles and degrees to the map at our feet.

We are travelling through this Canadian landscape overland, you are here to conduct your business, I saw you there in the ravine and I want to tell you about Djuna, how she is sitting on the hood, want to shout at you above the roar of wind tumbling in this open car as we fly past a rotten hedge where balances a Swainson's thrush.

Now the map's blue catches an echo of the sky as we note the cumulus advancing the horizon three degrees, and our darting eyes flit from floor to road to grey pond without lilies.

We're kicking up quite a dust just now, here, at this Canadian corner.

Tell me.

I move to Montreal. After Alice dies, I write Jeff telling him I am a lesbian. He writes back: Floods are not homosexuals. All right then, I think. Have it your way. I won't be a Flood except by silent adventure. I will sit in cafés drinking café au lait or absinthe. I will think thoughts and speak to no one.

There was a child went forth every day.
Start believing in time.

I have been walking all afternoon, trying to drown in the snow which falls in sheets. I have been walking all afternoon, rehearsing what I will say to Robin when I see her.

With Rae. My god. How could you do this to me? Every bed you leave, without caring, leaves you feeling peace and happiness. And now, once again, you think you have made your escape and you are free!

The snow is climbing the walls of the street, the light from front windows lies down like golden caskets cradled in the fresh snow. It is twilight. A lazy wind blows, gusting. It is Alice who would have called what is stabbing through my inadequate coat lazy: It goes through you instead of around you.

Lazy, Alice? It is hostile.

A shadow moves ahead of me. I can see it vaguely through heavy sweeping snow. It moves awkwardly through the blizzard. As I gain on the figure I can see an old woman leaning heavily on an elegant walking stick. *Djuna*. She wears her sturdy black pumps, and is unsuccessfully negotiating the slippery sidewalk. I hear her cursing, a deep contralto voice.

O, for chrissake. You damned fool, going out tonight of all nights. My god, it's dreadful. Dreadful.

I half expect her to suddenly vanish, just as she has done before, as Jeannette does, coming and going of her own accord, never when I beg her to appear. But Djuna continues to fuss even as I bear right down on top of her.

138

She turns, snapping at me.

All right, Nora, no need to climb up my back. Now let me take your arm, and let's get out of this dreadful snow. Come on now. Give me a hand.

Alarmed though I am to feel the real weight of human touch suddenly against my arm, I hold her as we make our way along St-Laurent toward home, Djuna complaining through the gusts that sometimes steal our breath.

You're not going to keep on with that dreadful woman, are you? she asks. Believe me, Nora, she'll break you. Don't I know. No, you don't want to show her a single thing more. My god! There's a beauty. How does she expect to invent anything? A person has to believe in something, Nora. Or someone. Believe in now. Here. Here. Everywhere. This is! Even cranky miserable old me had a little faith. One has to. I could not have invented you if my only purpose was to please myself. But that one! She's not on ground, she's on stone! No largesse. There's a part of that one she'll never give away. No, you just avoid them all, darling, and you'll be all right. I promise you. My god! Fools. The lot of them.

A cat flies past us and lands in a snowbank. Djuna screams, clapping her hand over her mouth. Then she begins to chuckle. She turns and looks at me, her eyes wide.

Listen, Nora, she says, the world is full of fools, you will keep meeting fools and then they get inside and you don't know the horror at the voices in your head when you get to be my age. But don't listen to fools. Listen to the sterile mind, if you can, that's the ticket. Do you understand? You must want to know what's here inside and out there.

Her finger traces an unspeakable line across my heart and then across the light breaking through.

Robin's trouble is that she imagines there is nowhere on God's green earth good enough for the likes of her stupendous talents. Nonsense. And you! You're full to the brim with pride. What words? Isn't that what your old pansy used to say? What words?

I don't know which way to go, Djuna! I cry.

Djuna points with her cane to a column of snow that gives the impression of rising rather than falling, and suddenly I am lifting out of my boots and rising into the air, pedalling, as in my dreams, on an inevitable bicycle, up through the falling snow into the dark sky, thousands of feet above the city. The lights below me sparkle, a grid of lights moving in discernible pattern across the landscape. I can see them through the veils of snow streaming alongside me as I am tossed on my uncertain course: The cross shimmering on the mountain, the Oratoire and the Olympic stadium. A host of dazed romantics flounder about in the maze of white streets circling the heart of the city. My ears begin to freeze and my toes turn hard as stone. I am turning, tossed in the wind, my skin opens flat like bedsheets breaking free from an ice-encrusted clothesline, sailing toward a frozen rose garden.

A tremendous knowledge overtakes me.

Djuna rises up out of her black pumps, she rises like a tiny black crow across the pale sky, she rises with her arms outstretched and all the lines upon her face washed clean, she is wearing a top hat, a white silk scarf about her elegant neck, she is wearing *un smoking*, her cheeks are rosy apples, a warm red life stains her full lips, she is rising, she is singing, she is exquisite, radiant, she is calling out to me, Nora, better to take one beautiful photograph than to make love all night long!

And when she passes through me, I begin my descent.

I am dropping down onto a darkened street in the Plateau, touching down on the sidewalk outside my apartment. Rae is there on the outer stairs. She is just leaving. Her little dog H.D. bounds away from her into the night.

H.D.! she calls. C'mere, girl! Hey, Nora. Is it you?

I try to speak to Rae, to ask her, How can you do this to me? but sound stays swirling like blood inside my mouth. The snow glows with its own inner light. Then, unexpectedly, something merges with this light and a great crimson heat breaks through the snow. I am standing barefoot on black ground, in Myra's garden, and the life of this garden beneath my feet is hollering.

Well, see you, Rae says, her eyes crawling around.

Drop by if you're in the neighbourhood.

I turn and head back to the Main. My feet, though white with the bite of snow, are warm. My boots stand on the sidewalk where I lifted out of them, the left one at a slight outward angle, the right one pointing straight ahead. Exactly my gait. A strange gaiety billows up in me as I spot Djuna sitting in a snowbank, her old wrinkled face returned to her, her thick legs pushed straight out in front of her, her unsteady hands clasped together in her lap, the walking stick jammed into the mound of snow beside her. She's catching a flood of snowflakes on her tongue. I decide I will not go home; instead I will ask Djuna to come to the studio, let me take her picture, then have a drink with me.

Now will you give up believing in time? she asks when she sees me. I stop dead in my tracks. What do you mean? I say, steeling myself to demand an explanation if she tries to evade my question but she is flattening into the relief of an old gold coin and rolling away.

I drink a lot of scotch and throw up a couple of times. I put black pen to page and draw parallel lines that refuse borders, circles that leave their centres, chevrons moving into zigzags. I hold the Nikon away from my shimmering body and take my own picture. I take away the light on the surfaces of things and hold a candle in the dark, creating looming shadows. Open the lens and wait, let the moment record its passing, don't worry; it comes slanting like time through a heart taking heed of itself.

This morning I curl like a cat curls around a wood stove, curl around my self, my hand breaking the space between my thighs. As if I had known to do this just then a gush of blood comes into my cupped hand. I am holding my own blood in my hand under three blankets and a star that gives no light.

I run blind to the bathroom. The cat stumbles after me, blinking dumbly. It is six am.

I wash my hand, my blood running pink into the basin, swirling. I move into the living room. I can see my vulva if I drop from my waist — I am falling. My ass is bare and smooth and vulnerable. The smell of ancient blood grows in the burning fire's heat. I miss Robin then. I crawl back into bed.

I imagine her: Tight, standing in the middle of a room, rocking from foot to foot, blind. I mumble Fuck out loud, the cramping is getting worse. Watch the colour come into the slanting clouds, grey at first coming pink. I watch the window, watch the newly fallen snow come pink come into blood come into blue. I want purple and something else that won't come. I feel sick.

My mouth tastes like baking soda after I throw up. I rinse the plastic basin of my vomit then get back into bed, wondering again if Robin will come home at all. I wish I had said, What will you do without me? but I made a big scene the night before about giving me time (my blood cupped in my hand alone), a golden suitcase jerking across the floor. What if the world counted on me to know myself? A fragment from a dream about adolescence, mine, the quality of skin like my ass, a beautiful thing.

I make coffee. While water blasts up through the grounds, I tie my blood around words in my head like sacred documents, my words bleached and quick and needing her ear, a thousand racing words about what it could be like, leaving her. Line them up on the edge of a razor blade. I keep a quick pace, waiting for reason to come, but every bend reproduces my old closet and banished candle, voices battling, claws under the door. The only way is forward, scratching pith and pulp, pulling back raw flesh, bending my head to observe how Robin's tongue slowly protrudes, how she moves it on a dark nipple, how the tongue scratches slightly, how the body rises. Observing Robin tearing off clothes, jamming dildo into harness into another, tongues in strange darkness, the heat of new skin the hook of an anchor she needs.

There is nothing I will not bend to see. No story I wish to prevent the telling of. Running behind with an open notebook, a Nikon camera if not her heart. A lifetime of shadow and light to explore if I give up believing in time.

But there are no ends to the earth. For forty years Djuna carried stones in her pockets. Waiting. What was the purpose of forty-odd years drunk in a bachelor apartment on Patchin Place? Could she make no use of Nothing? Why invent me, then?

The bait rises up in the night, roaring, and I take it.

Where the heart opens, that is the Way.

You are shooting photographs in a famous restaurant on St-Denis when a woman comes up to you asking, Can I take your picture?

Yes. And no one will believe it, you answer. I look like a small brown bird. We Are All Like This.

You wait for Robin.

You have begun the excavation. The stranger you unearth has a solar plexus full of diamonds. There are pebbles in her mouth. The trajectory of desire is a cool stone thrown, and when it lands you know: You are leaving to go somewhere.

I wrote Myra a note today, just a hello to let her know I am alive and that I am thinking about her. Robin said, Just love her for an hour here and there. But loving

Myra and the others is a lot like taking a picture. I have to practice. Call myself a practitioner. I can't just turn it on and off. It requires long preparation in my mind and self-examination in my skin. Bodies in infinity is what I'm trying to stand.

I regret all those years I didn't believe in my loving, but then I tell myself, Forget it.

Do it now.

Don't waste your time.

The community that I begin to photograph is full of contradictions and nuances, is a sick and gorgeous, a treacherous and glorious, thing.

After Robin leaves for work, after I unpack the suitcase and put it back into the closet; when the memory of last night's cruelties have me crawling on my knees, unable to lift my head; when the hour that follows this is darker still, I take my camera and admit escape. Next to me at a marble-top table in this Montreal café of cool teal and dark terra cotta is a dyke. She is young, strong. Head-hugger of a crew cut with a slash of long white hair tucked behind one ear, her claim to former crisis. She is wearing a short army jacket, black jeans rolled up twice neatly at the ankles. Green socks. Converse sneakers.

Does she smoke? Yes. Look. Inconspicuously. The smoke drifts up from her hand where it dangles below the table between her legs. She is reading *Voir*.

Does she wear black lingerie to seduce a lover? Does she wear her runners? Are her strong legs coated with a fine captivating down? Does she change behind the bathroom door or above her lover on the bed? Does she wear a dildo, slide carefully into her date?

Does she hate sex, preferring instead her John Players in their shining black box?

Does she sense me watching? Does the impulse to speak overtake her? Would she like to run?

What colour are her eyes?

Has her father just died? Is her mother —

Is she hungry? Does she like to travel?

Is she H I V positive? Does she speak English?

Has she ever loved a man?

What colour are her eyes?

When she looks at herself in a mirror does she wink?

What does she do for cash?

Can she tell herself much she needs to hear?

Has she ever tried to kill herself?

Did she take music lessons when she was young?

Has she ever held a gun?

Has she ever had a stranger hold a cool cloth to her hot forehead while she puked into a bowl?

Does she believe in everlasting life?

I dream I am climbing around dark streets looking for a guillotine. Robin is fucking two women in a church. On my prowl I run into Donny. I tell him about Robin. He tells me, The life of the mind is only an effort to hide the body so the teeth don't stick out. I ask him is he quoting? He says, Forget Robin, and make up some rules of your own.

Is there a way to foster a new realm of dreams? Surely indifference has no territory in the heart. Only voluptuous deep loving solitude, the lost moment of travelling imagination? The open aperture and a view of the world?

Your love when it began was fit to dry a rose in. Now a window has broken and petals scurry along the baseboards. A window isn't broken but a door blows away.

How long can you balance on the fulcrum of a lie?

You are tracking light as it moves across the world. Your photos hang from tacks around your studio; you lean your back up against the brick wall and study the sequence taken yesterday: The dyke in the small café.

Maybe we spend our whole lives garnering love. In yesterday's photos, the citizens of the world experiment with their lives. Who tried to leave the sterile heart; who made things worse for their loved ones by speaking the words, It is over; who stayed on in sadness and anger; who jumped from a seventh-floor window?

You wonder if the love Robin says she has for you will last without a home. You go to the window of your studio, deck yourself out, dance, laugh: Then throw it all away.

I am meeting Robin tonight for dinner at Le Continental, she is treating me to pasta alla carbonara, she will taunt me as the raw egg begins to tilt then spill its alchemy over the steaming spaghettini. She will laugh, throw back her long elegant neck. She will regain her focus, lean in toward me, pour more wine.

You look so alive, she will say.

ACKNOWLEDGEMENTS

The author gratefully acknowledges financial support from the Canada Council for the Arts, the Ontario Arts Council and the City of Toronto through the Toronto Arts Council. In addition, the author wishes to acknowledge the ongoing vital debate from which she benefits within her Toronto literary community. Thanks in particular to Chris Chambers and Derek McCormack, inimitable hearts and minds.

Heartfelt thanks to Alana Wilcox for her careful reading of the manuscript and her generous and intelligent suggestions for its improvement. Deepest gratitude also to Rachel Vigier and Jennifer Glossop, and to Diana Thorneycroft for the use of her striking photograph.

Loving thanks to Zab for her unfailing artful vision, to Justine Pimlott, Jay Koornstra and Tsipi Raber for enduring friendship, and to Vanessa Pandos for providing a beautiful corner of the world in which to finish the book.

Most telling thanks to Chris Chambers, for trueness and beauty and everything connected by 'and' and 'and.'

E.A. HOBART

BETH FOLLETT is the publisher and in-house editor of Pedlar Press, an independent literary press. She lives in Toronto.

To read the online version of this text and other titles from
Coach House Books, visit our website:
www.chbooks.com

To add your name to our e-mailing list, write:
mail@chbooks.com

COACH HOUSE BOOKS
401 Huron Street (rear) on bpNichol Lane
Toronto, Ontario
M5S 2G5

TOLL-FREE 1-800-367-6360